THE REUNION

THE REUNION

It was supposed to be a ten year reunion but soon became their worst nightmare!

ANAS KAMAL

Anecdote
Publishing House

Anecdote
Publishing House

Anecdote Publishing House
E-35-A, E Block, Gali No. 2, Ganesh Nagar,
Pandav Nagar Complex, Delhi - 110092

Published by Anecdote Publishing House

First Edition 2022

Second Edition 2024

ISBN: 9788195251889

MRP: ₹ 299.00

Book Promoted and Marketed by Champ Readers Pvt. Ltd.
Edited by Swati Vijay
Layout and Cover by Aamir Ali
Printed by Thomson Press, India

Dedicated to my brother.

&

Dedicated to myself for not giving up after all that happened.

I am Proud of Myself.

Chapter - 1

It was Monday morning when the letter arrived on her doorstep. Shreya was ready to leave home, to get to her new home. She is unemployed for the last two months; all she did to get fired, was to shout in front of the company's gate, drunk. She wasn't like this always. She was a nice, cute, and smart girl. Good in academics, since she learned to read. But after the incident, her life changed, she wasn't herself anymore. She started drinking, breaking laws, speed driving, and doing other harmful stuff.

She even was finally moving away from her best friend. They have both been roommates for a long time. But she thought it wouldn't be good to live there, any longer, so for a couple of past few weeks, she started looking for an apartment. She needed some place alone, far away without any roommate.

But the single rooms were costly and she was living on her savings, for who knows how long.

She finally found an apartment, away from both her old living and working places. It was only one room, but that's all she could get within budget. She was ready to go, all packed and set, she chose Monday, so her friend would not be at home and she won't have to face her. It's not that she was angry at her or something; she just wasn't in the mood for a casual goodbye. In reality, she just couldn't see her face, or she won't be able to leave.

As she hung her keys on the hanger and opened the door, she turned around for a final look. So many years, so many memories were alive at this place. She could somehow, see all of them in front of her like a movie. Her eyes got moist. She turned to leave and saw an envelope, as she picked it up and turned towards the written side. She saw a familiar monogram, it was from her school. She had spent all her childhood at that same school. She had now forgotten about her school, it was there in her mind but buried deep down. That came out of the blue, after a glimpse of that letter. She turned back and sat, the letter said….

Liberty Public Sr. Sec. School,
1254, Karol Bagh,
Delhi-110005

Dear Alumni,

We hereby inform you that the school committee has organized a reunion of the 10th standard, batch 2010. The reunion will be held at the school premises on 12 November 2021. You are very much invited to the reunion. We are informing you in a week advance, so you could finish all your work and come enjoy.

If you are coming, please send us a confirmation R.S.V.P. on our school email id Libertykarolbagh.headoffice@gmail.com.

All of your friends will be there, and it will be a two-day event. Stay, food, and everything else is on us. You just come and enjoy. Come and see how much has changed in the past ten years, and how much you have changed. Some of our students are lawyers, engineers, doctors, writers, journalists, etc. But back then you all were just kids, trying to pass out exams, playing on the ground, and talking to your friends all day about, God knows what. Rekindle your inner child again and go back in time when you were small and used to wear uniforms.

We will be waiting for you.

Still Principal
Gautam Bhatia

For a moment, she didn't move, so much had happened in the past ten years. It was a big decision for her, especially at that time, to go or not. She did not want to meet her friends, who were all successful and happy, in their lives. Not that she was jealous, but just it wasn't the right time for a reunion.

She folded the letter, put it in her bag, and finally left.

Chapter - 2

As he reached home from work, Mayank saw a letter on the porch. After seeing the monogram, his feelings were a little different. A smile came on his face from ear to ear. The letter took him a decade back when he was nobody. Not someone, the teachers, or other fellow students would remember if he suddenly had died, he used to think that. He was what you say a loser, a kid all other kids used to bully. He did not go to school much, because he was annoyed and frustrated and still couldn't do anything.

Kids used to pick on him, would slap him for no reason, and make fun of him almost every day. He was from a poor family; his father had died before he could speak. His mother, grandmother, and grandfather were all he had; he was a nice kid when he was little. But as puberty hit him, he didn't grow tall as normally boys do. He was stuck at the height of 5ft., with a thin structure and pale color. Because of his size and structure, his school life was not something he would want to remember.

But now the circumstances had changed; now he has a big business. Those things changed him and made him a better person. He was still in the same in looks, but he dropped out of school because of the abuse, after that incident. His whole life was changed, he left in the middle of the 10th standard, just before the board exams were about to begin. Some days, he would just sit alone in his room and not talk to anyone, even his grandfather, he had a very good relationship with him; he was like a father and a friend to him.

Then after a couple of weeks of sitting alone, he one day suddenly left home and returned with news, that he would work at the garage near his home. His family couldn't understand the reason for the sudden change but they were finally happy, seeing him happy. His mother tried to hug him; he stopped her in the middle and let his grandfather hug him. He was so happy that he cried a little.

After that, he never looked back, worked his ass off at the garage, learned everything, and two or three years later opened one of his own. He still worked tirelessly for the next five years and opened his car showroom of Maruti Suzuki, and now he has 5 car showrooms all over Delhi NCR. He got a big house, bigger than he ever thought he would have. His family had never been so happy and proud of him, before.

This was the reason behind his smile. Now he will show them what he has. He read the letter and instantly sent his confirmation mail. It was going to be the best reunion ever because he had something special in his mind.

Chapter - 3

She got the letter a little late. Her father had a textile business and she was his only child, now you can imagine she had a very promising childhood. Riya was the star kid of her school, all-time topper, and debate and spelling bee champion. She won first prize in an essay writing competition at the national level. She was every teacher's favorite and every kid wanted to be her friend. She had her girl gang, there were three of them and all three of them were smart, beautiful, and in demand. She got everything easily; she was a princess of her own little world.

Now she was a teacher at an elementary school near her house. Her new house was at Loni, Ghaziabad. So many things had happened in the past 10 years; her father's business started declining. He had to mortgage his house and he lost his sponsors. He finally took a big loan for his business and failed to pay. He lost his business and his house, from a 5 BHK; they were now living in a one-room flat near her current house.

Things changed after she completed her education in teaching and got a job, which she was still doing. In some years, their financial situation changed but her father couldn't get over the loss and left her and her mother alone. Her mother waited for her father sitting in front of the door, but he never returned. She finally moved on after some years when she got too ill to sit there.

The letter brought back so many memories, good ones. Not so good now, time had changed everything. Painful memories changed into subjects of laugh and, happy memories begin to hurt as the moment passed by. She was not going to attend the reunion; she put the letter away and went to the bathroom. She had just returned from school and soon there will be children all over her place because she gives tuition.

As the clock struck at 3:00 pm, and she had just finished her lunch. Children started to come; her place was filled with screaming, shouting kids. She was used to this but today because of the letter she was little disturbed. Saransh was a naughty kid, who was not so good at studies but was very smart. His parents were a bit overprotective and over concerned, and they eat brains, not literally. She was in no mood to meet them and gave them a two-hour lecture about his progress which they will not understand because they would be busy telling his complaints, about how he doesn't study at home and watch cartoons all the time. How she should give more attention to him. Then Saransh informed her that they will come next week.

After two hours of screaming and shouting at kids at a particular decibel the word “Silence”. She sat down on her bed and switched off her table lamp, put her head on the bed, and slowly her eyes shut down. She started dreaming that her mother was on the deathbed and she was holding her hand just the moment before her death. She was crying and said to her “My child, all my life was devoted to your father and then to two of you. I have no regrets but there is one thing that I would have liked if it had gone as I wanted. I wanted to grow old with your father and die in his arms; I wanted him to love me, to express his love towards me. He never did, when his business was good, he was busy in it, then when it declined he threw all his attention and focus into saving it. I never got his love. My only advice to you is to live your life in your way and be happy, love someone who loves you.” Then she died and suddenly she woke up to only see her mother’s photo frame on the wall, in front of her with a garland over it.

She was too busy, trying to improve her life, her finances, complete her education, and find a job as soon as possible. But there was a boy she liked back at her school time; she thought it would be a good chance to meet him again at the reunion. But then she thought, he would have gotten married by now, there is no good in going. But there was something a spark lit inside her after a long time, a spark of hope, and at that moment, she knew she was going to the reunion.

Chapter - 4

There she was standing with a bottle in her hand, and the label on it said "Rat Poison". Suddenly, the doorbell rang; hesitatingly she put it aside and opened the door. There was Mrs. Ahuja, standing in front of her "I collected it because you were not at home, Maya, it came for you and it says 'URGENT'", she said and handed over the letter. Maya said "Thank you" and closed the door. The letter had "URGENT" written on it at the front, in big red letters slightly tilted to the left. She threw it away on the sofa; she knew what was in it. It was her unpaid electricity bill that was due over three months. She did not need to see it again. As she moved toward the bottle, she saw an envelope on the ground near her foot; she picked it up and saw a familiar monogram. She remembered it pretty well.

Lots of memories were attached to it, some good and some bad. But she was in no mood to remember them. Still, she opened it, on reading the letter, Reunion was not something that was on her mind at that time. She opened the bottle and put some pills in her hand, and was about to eat them but she suddenly threw them away. Death was not something, she wanted, she wanted to live. She had been a very happy-go-lucky person all her life, at least till last year. Everything fell apart last year after her husband's death; she went into depression and quit everything, even her job. All she did, was just sit on the bed all day, sometimes lying down crying, holding her husband's picture.

Her parents wanted her to come back to Delhi, to their home. But she was so attached to her house, she declined the offer. She even didn't let them come, to take care of her but they came anyway and, had just left a couple of days back. They kept sending her some money every month for her expenses. She wanted to stay there, at her home, and do nothing. She loved him very much, and he loved her back. They were the, what you say an "Ideal Couple". Everyone was jealous of them, as their friends used to say.

They had a love marriage; they fell in love at college. They got married just two years back but had not had a child yet, but were planning on having one. They first wanted to settle down and have a stable income, a good house before having a child. He died in the third wave of Corona. That broke her to the soul, she just fell apart.

The reunion letter reminded her of her best friends and the fun, they used to have back then. She knew death was not an answer for the pain, she needed to live. He would have wanted that too. She thought it would be a change of environment and people after a very long time, which she needed the most. She thought by meeting her friends and relieving her old days with them, will probably help her to get back to life. She threw the bottle in the trash and sent the confirmation mail right away before she had a change of mind. Now she was going and deep down somewhere in that recently turned cold heart, was still some warmth left. Hope to live.

Chapter - 5

"Raviiiii... a letter came for you", said his mom screaming from the kitchen.

"What Ma...! Why do you always shout so much?"
"Shut up, already you have been sitting on your ass since you got fired, in an age where I should be taking care of Bahu; I have to take care of you."
"How many times...you are going to remind me of that?"
"Why don't you go out...and search for a job?"
"Tell me... why you were shouting my name?"
"Here...! This letter came for you..."
"Okay..."
"What is it...?" she asked.
"How would I know, I can't see through things...let me read first!"
"Hmm..."

He went into his room which was now converted into half room/ half gym. It used to be a fully functional room when he had a job to pay for the gym, now this is all he's got. A couple of weights, dumbbells, rods, not much just normal stuff. He always had been a gym freak since he was 18. He still has the looks, a well-built physique, broad shoulders, wide chest, and the best jaw line you would have seen in Hollywood movies.

At school, he was a basketball champion and captain of the school team. He was a star kid, every girl's dream boyfriend. Every guy wanted to be his friend to become popular. He wanted to become a full-time basketball player, but life had a plan of its own. He got into an accident and broke his leg; he was advised not to play ever again. That broke his heart but because of family pressure, he did M.com and worked as an accountant for a couple of years until he got fired.

He didn't want to go, but it was a good chance to leave his house for a while and also to get away from his mother's tantrums and sarcasm. He told his mother that he has to go for the reunion. "What...what reunion?" she asked in haste. "School reunion, ma..." he answered and closed his room's door, behind him.

At School

Everyone reached school on time. After a very long time, all five of them were there. They didn't talk or even looked at each other, straight went into the school. There were all of the faces, which once they were used to be familiar with. But along with some new faces. The place was already full of people roaming here and there; it was all decorated with balloons and posters of 90s rock bands and pictures of the students on multiple occasions. A big banner on the wall opposite the entry gate, says "Welcome Class", as they walked further there were snacks on tables around them and also some beer cans.

They thought there will be someone to welcome them, but there was no one; it was expected, because their school was never good at organizing events. One time on Diwali, they organized a dance competition, at which there was no sound system. At the last moment, the provider declined to deliver it due to some issue with school management. So they instead had a drawing competition that day, all students were in their costumes, sitting on the ground, making drawings.

So it was nothing they weren't used to. The decorations were done, but the speed of staff members going here and there was showing that some things were still under work. There were chairs in the middle of the assembly ground, where they all sat. Nobody looked at each other directly, but some glimpses were exchanged along with some fake smiles. Someone had to break the ice, or it was going to be an awkward silence, looking at your crush-like scenario, where you look at your crush from the corner of your eyes, but not directly.

A lot had happened in the past decade, they were in touch for a couple of years in the beginning, but as life happened they lost touch with each other. Ohh, sorry I forgot to tell you that they all were good friends once, best of friends you could say at that time. They were together from the beginning of their teenage years, till they all completed school.

So many memories were there, waiting to be recalled. In between the rush of people, they felt like sitting in the middle of the desert, just five of them, trying to avoid an awkward conversation. "Hey... how are you all guys?" a voice came from the right corner; they all turned towards the voice. It was their principal, who had finally come to greet them. They all said 'Hellos' but didn't talk to each other.

"I am fine..." said Ravi.

"Good..." said Shreya with her cute smile.

"I am good too" replied Mayank and Maya, surprisingly at the same time, I guess it happened because of their old habit, back when were kids, somehow being in the same place their subconscious minds picked up an old setting for a moment. Riya didn't answer; she was lost in her thoughts.

"So the gang is finally back together, after so long...that too at their old home ground!" said the principal, laughing nervously, maybe by that time he had anticipated that they were not interested in a conversation.

"Yeah, it's good to be back" Shreya replied.

"Yupp...How are you, sir? You haven't changed a bit in ten years..." said Ravi jokingly.

"It's not like that, I am older now...!" said the principal, while blushing like a little girl. "Yeah, you haven't changed a bit..." said Mayank and then said "You were bald from always..." in a whisper and laughed silently.

"What...did you say something?"

"No… nothing!"

"Ohh…okay"

"So are you guys ready for the fun...? For the next two days...!"

"Yuppp, we are all very excited...!" said Shreya, and all you could see on their faces were grave smiles.

"So, you guys make yourselves comfortable, I have to go...!"

"Carry on, Sir don't let us come is your way..." Ravi said with a handshake.

"Seriously...! A handshake..." Shreya said looking at him.

"I couldn't think of anything else, it's not like he was my best buddy," Ravi said in his defence. "It's still better from what he said...!" Ravi said pointing towards Mayank.

"What? What did I say wrong, he was bald from the beginning...." said Mayank and finally the awkward silence

turned into something cheerful and they all laughed. After so long, laughing together at their silly doings, they felt so good. Even, Riya joined them this time, she couldn't stop herself.
"So what you guys have been up to these days...?" asked Ravi.
"Just usual, day-to-day life... home then office..." replied Shreya. "Yeah nothing special," said Mayank and Riya. Maya always had been a joyful girl, but there was strange silence on her face. Still, she replied casually "Just daily housework, you know, as a typical housewife....".
"Yeah, you got married I heard, congratulations...!" said Ravi in a happy voice. Suddenly Maya's face went blank, for a moment she just zoned out. "So, how was it?" asked Shreya.
"Huh…what?" she said in response.
"I was asking how your marriage was; it must have been big, huh..."
"Yeah, it was pretty awesome, and thank you, Ravi...!"
"Ohh… you heard me, I thought I was ignored!" Ravi said and laughed.

"No, it's not like that. I was just thinking something...".
"You must be missing your husband, the first time this far away from him," Shreya said and giggled. "Yeah, I was..." Maya said in a low voice. "It's just two days, he will be fine, don't worry. I am sure he can survive for two days, without his dear wife...". "Yeah..." she replied and laughed non-heartedly.
"So what do you do, Shreya?" Maya asked before, Shreya could ask any further questions. "I work at Fashion4U; I am head of the Fashion and innovation department". "Wow, it's a big fashion magazine, you must be pretty busy..." said Maya.

"What do you do? Ravi...!" Shreya asked diverting the attention from her. "I work at a firm, as an accountant," he said with a little smile. "That's good, what firm?"Maya asked. "At DMR associates", he told her the name of the firm he used to work at, he just couldn't think of any other name so sudden. "Mayank, what you do bro?" Ravi said, this time diverting attention from him.

"I have my own business, multiple car showrooms all over Delhi", he said with a smile, this time a real one. "Ohh... So you are loaded, man". "No, not like that!" Mayank said. "Don't tell me that it's your car parked outside, that silver Mercedes?" he said with a surprised and excited face. "Yeah, it's mine". "Bro, you have Mercedes Benz and you are telling me, you are not loaded". "It seems pretty new" he added. "Yeah, I just bought it last month". And everyone congratulated him. They all were pretending, they were happy and satisfied with their lives, telling lies about their work, family and houses. No one told the truth to the other.

"What about you, Riya?" everyone turned towards her. "Me…I just work at an MNC, nothing special...!" she said with a fake smile. "Wow that's pretty awesome, so you are still your father's princess..." asked Mayank.
"Yeah, but now I live separate at my own house."

"That's great, you bought a house on your own" Ravi said with excitement. "Yeah, it's not that big, just 1500 sq. ft." "Holy shit 1500 and you are saying it's not that big, well, probably you are right because you are used to living in big houses since you were born," said Ravi again in excitement. "How's your father's business been doing?" asked Maya and Mayank.

Chapter - 6

"So guys, today we are going to recall old memories, and tomorrow we will be having a dance night... the day after that will be a gift ceremony because you all put your work at a halt and came here. Also, there will be other activities as well with food and beverages, so don't shy, Enjoy...!"

That was the opening speech of Principal. The other batchmates had come by afternoon and they all were standing in the auditorium, in their separate groups, old friends had found each other and were now gossiping about the time lost. All three sections of class tenth were present there. And our gang was also standing with beer cans in their hands. "What is it with Astha mam, she didn't come?" said somebody. "I heard that she got divorced recently, maybe that's why" someone else replied. "That was supposed to happen, no man could bear her," said someone and they all laughed.

"You heard, they are talking about Astha mam, that she got divorced!" Ravi said in the group, whispering. "So what, it's her personal matter...none of our business," Shreya said in an angry tone. "Okay, firey tornado, don't get angry, I was just saying...". "Don't call me by that name". "Why we used to call you by this, all the time, remember!" he said and they all laughed.

"Let's go outside," said Shreya.
"But what about the reunion!"
"This is our reunion... not the school's, we can celebrate it outside too!"
"Okay, let's go!"
"But the Principal just said, there are going to recall memories," said Maya, looking worried. "They will probably show us some old videos, of our classes dancing or doing something else, I have already seen them once and don't want to watch them again," said Shreya insistently. "Yeah, she is right, let's go..." said Mayank. "What you say Riya?" asked somebody. "I am ready, let's go!" she said pointing towards the exit.

"Come, Maya, it will be better than here...".
"Okay fine let's go..." she said and turned towards the exit. "Where do you think you are going?" said Ravi stopping her by hand. "Out?". "There will be a guard, who will not let us go outside...". "So, what you all say, Old Valley?" said Ravi with a naughty smile.
"You still remember it!" said Shreya and Maya.

"Don't you?"

"Let's go out guys, like good old days". They left in the crowd, without anyone knowing.

"It's supposed to be here, right?"

"Yeah, I don't think it could have moved..."

"But, where is it, I can't find..."

"Move, let me see! They were in the canteen back at school, when they were in seventh or eighth, they found a secret passage that goes all the way from under the wall of the school to the other side at an old ground.

"It should be here..."

"See, as I said, it's not there...!"

"Do you think they filled it after we were gone?"

"Maybe..."

"It could be possible..."

"Look, you idiots it's here not there...!" said Mayank, pointing towards the passage.

"What! We all were looking at the wrong place" said Ravi laughingly.

"It's been so long, we forgot," said the girls, also laughing. They moved the rock; underneath it was a small tunnel.

"Would we be able to fit in it?"

"Let's find out."

"I will go first!" said Ravi.

"Like always, go..." said Mayank with a smile.

"Guys, I am stuck!"

"Good..." said Mayank and they all laughed wholeheartedly.

"Don't just stand there and laugh, do something...!"

"That's the price you have to pay in return to look like

Arnold...!" said Riya and they giggled.
"Don't start crying, I am coming" said Mayank. He kicked him from behind until he got out on the other side. Then they all came behind him.
"Guys see this!"
"Woah, so much has changed in ten years...!"
"Wasn't here used to be an old ground..."
"Yeah, but look at it now, totally changed..."
"Yeah, it's a park now, with grass in place of sand and stones..."
"Look, they also got swings and other rides!"
"Yeah and benches too!"
"Let's sit here for a while..."
"Okay"

Chapter - 7

"It looks good guys, the living arrangements...!"
"Yeah, it feels good too," said Ravi. They all were sitting in one of the classes; there were mattresses on the floor. The arrangement was that students will sleep in classes for the night.
"You remember, how we used to talk about sleeping at school, I never thought it would happen someday...!"
"I think you wanted to spend some quality time Mayank," said Ravi and elbowed Mayank.
"Shut up".
"Sorry," he said and they laughed while Maya was trying to beat him.
"Joke aside, she is right we all wanted to spend a night at school..." said Riya.
"Yeah, it feels like a dream come true".
"So, what did we want to do on our night stay at school?"

"We wanted to talk about ghosts and tell horror stories to each other".
"So, let's do it".
"Now?"
"Then when will we get another chance to do it?"
"Yeah, it's a good idea".
"Let's do it," all said in union.
"So, who wants to go first?"
"I will," said Ravi.

So it starts like this....

Long ago there was a princess, so beautiful that there was no one near her in all the four kingdoms of Orasin. She was the only daughter of the king and the single heir to the throne. She did not want to get married, but her father and mother wanted that. They had shown her multiple princess from other kingdoms, but she liked no one. One day she was out walking with her friends, when she saw a handsome man of her age on a white horse. At that exact moment, she felt something, she had never felt before. She felt love, for someone other than family and friends. The man had come to meet her father. After he went inside; she went near his horse which was standing in front, with a royal guard. She asked him about the man, he said he don't know him. He had seen him the first time around this place. She asked him how did he let him go inside, then. He told her that he had the seal of Aurus with him.

She followed him intended to find out who was he, he went straight into the jungle and just disappeared into thin air. She searched for a while but found no sign of him. She returned and asked her father, he said it was something he couldn't discuss with her. That night she slept thinking of him and woke up in the middle of the night, to a loud sound of a thud. She went near her window but saw no one, strangely no one was there, the palace was emptier than usual. There should be guards standing and torches lit but it was dark and empty. She went out without making a noise or coming into someone's sight.

She straight went into the dark forest, then when she was about to return. She heard a noise and followed it; it was coming from somewhere deep in the forest. As she moved closer to the sound, the sound was now recognizable but strange, it was like someone was gnawing bones. She got scared but couldn't control her curiosity and walked ahead. What she saw there was so evil and horrifying for her, she lost consciousness. When she woke up the next day, she tried to understand what she was doing there. Then it suddenly came back to her, the horrific evil scene of last night. She gulped and started sweating, she stood up and went straight back to the palace and told no one what happened or what she saw that night.

"What type of bullshit story is that?" said Mayank and threw a pillow on Ravi.

"Yeah, what was it, I thought you were telling us a horror story!" said Riya and Shreya, Maya was still confused about what to say or did she missed something in the story.

"Wait… guys, let me tell you what she saw first, then tell me how is the story..."

"Okay, go ahead," said everyone, feeling excited again.

"She saw her father and that man, eating what looked like remains of a person..."

"Holy shit, I didn't see that coming...!"

"But why?"

"I don't know, maybe they were trolls or some other dark creatures, living between humans or they were just cannibals, who used to live in the forest, those days."

"That was a pretty strange story, less of a story more of a puzzle..." said Riya.

"That's how a good story should be!" said Ravi with a smile.

Riya

Let me apologize if you didn't get the story. Don't worry, we too didn't understand it. That is how it always has been with Ravi's stories, whenever he tried to tell us a story in our free periods, we never got it, but he didn't seem to care about it too. He just enjoys telling stories. When we were in school, he wanted to become a writer but couldn't write a simple essay. We made fun of him about it, often. Maybe that's why he forgot about his this passion and started working as an accountant.

Mayank and Maya always seemed to like each other, but they never said anything, neither of them. We, and by we, I mean Shreya and me, were close back then, we used to study together and hang out, other than the group, just two of us. She was the only person who understood me better than anyone else. We just had a connection, maybe because both of our parents were well-to-do or you could say we were princesses, who had everything they needed, as Ravi and Mayank used to say. But whatever the reason it was, we were good friends, after my father's business broke down. I started to hang out less with her, I was ashamed of my father's failure, or maybe I was just not ready to accept, that the only thing we had in common "Money", was no longer a common denominator.

I lost contact with her soon after school finished. She was a nice girl; she would have never let this thing come, into our friendship. But I was afraid that she might. Soon we became strangers from best of friends, and just like that, we all went our way. We used to gossip about everything for hours, including the unaccepted love of Maya and Mayank. We sometimes tried to ask Maya, you know the girl on girl talk. She never admitted it. I got to know from our other girl friends, that Ravi also confronted Mayank about this; well you know gossip travels faster in a school than in a country. Much faster between teenagers and soon, everyone was talking about their love and relationship, which made both of them embarrassed and shy. They started to go out less together, except when all of us were together.

Ravi and Mayank fought with a couple of boys, who were teasing Mayank. Shreya and I also fought with some bitches of our class and even got physical, when they tried to harass Maya. I also used to like Ravi; he was smart and handsome and had a very good jaw line, which he still seems to have. I never told anyone about this, not even Shreya. I was afraid of his reaction, but I was more afraid of us becoming a hot topic of gossip at school. I had to act smart more after the events with Maya and Mayank so that anyone wouldn't find out about this. Even Ravi had no idea, about my feelings for him, to this day.

Chapter - 9

It "You remember we used to come here every day after school..." said Ravi. They all were drinking tea at a tea shop nearby, there was a breakfast arrangement at school, but they wanted to rekindle their friendship.

"Yeah, how can I forget!" said Shreya with a smile, looking at Riya for approval.

"Yeah, I remember it when you fell right in front of that sewer..." said Mayank with a big laugh.

"Yeah, like you got caught while trying to steal *Matthi*, from Rama Bhai...!"

"Yeah I remember that too...!" said Rama, the tea shop owner while stirring tea.

"I wasn't trying to steal, I would have paid you for that but you caught me first, I was just taking it to eat..."

"Yeah, spoke Raja Harish Chandra, the always truth-teller...!" said Riya and gave Maya and Shreya a high-five.

"Don't you say anything, I know when you stole notes of

Kavita mam, so she wasn't able to take the class that day..." said Ravi with a wink.

"It was you, damn girl...!"

"How do you know?"

"I saw you going into the staff room and coming back with some papers, which I understood were what when Kavita mam started searching for it everywhere and then told us to come out... if we had anything to do with that!"

"You did good, you should have told us!" said Shreya.

"Yeah, like I told you about the affair of Suman mam and physical education sir... I don't remember his name! And you told everyone about it!"

"Wait, wait, when did that happen, how come I don't know...?" asked Mayank.

"How would you know stupid... you were in a different section and it happened in ours..." all four of them replied.

"Ohh… yeah, sorry I used to hang out so much with you guys, I usually forget that I was in another section..."

"Yeah, you seemed to have no friends from your class, but why?"

"They were all stupid, and I am not saying you all are not, but they were stupider...!"

"Shut up!!"

"*Chai* is still the same as it used to be ten years ago..." said Shreya sipping from the cup.

"Yeah, that's the magic of Rama Bhai, hell I missed it man...!" said Ravi.

"Yeah, same old taste, same old friends. It feels like nothing had changed..."

"Well! something has changed, you are more fat now...!" said Ravi to Maya.

"Shut up, I am not fat...!"

"Yeah, she is not fat Ravi... people tend to put on a little weight. it is a sign of happy married life..." said Shreya and elbowed Maya.

"It's not like that..." Maya replied in a low voice.

"Don't tease her, you guys..." said Mayank.

"Look who spoke...!" Ravi said and they all laughed out loud.

Chapter - 10

"So, what are you going to wear tonight?"
"I don't know, I have nothing to wear for an occasion like dance night...!" said Riya, trying multiple dresses, standing in front of a mirror that was held by Maya. They were in another classroom, which was set aside as a changing room for girls. Boys were busy bathing, because there was a long queue in front of the temporary set bathroom by the college.
"Enough yaar, I am done waiting...!" said Mayank, getting frustrated.
"So, what do you want to do instead, skip bath...!" Ravi said with a wink.
"I wish we could, like when we were kids" Mayank laughed.
"You used to not bathe, I knew it...!"
"How?"
"One day, I saw dogs came near you sniffing..."
"You bastard!!!" said Mayank and gave him a head rub.
"Stop it!"
"Let's go to *Tanki*..."

"*Tanki* ...! You remember it...!"
"Yeah, I do..."
"Then, let's go!"

They left the waiting line and went out to a place near there, it was a water tank, at least it was supposed to be, but it never got that chance. So the boys used to use it as their water war zone, they used to go there sometimes after school. Play with water from the nearby tap, which they would connect with a piece of plastic pipe. They used to play there all afternoon when the heat used to be on top. And during summer vacations, they would play with water-filled balloons till the sun came down. It was the good old days, no tension, no worries only limitless fun.

"It's still here, I can't believe it...!"
"Yeah, me too!"
"So many memories, alive at this place, so many fun afternoons and fights..."
"Yeah, I miss those days, now that I remember it..."
"But so much has changed..."
"It doesn't look like, as I remember it!"
"It wasn't supposed to, it's been ten years now," said Mayank. They were standing in front of an old iron gate, rusted and broken a little. There was a strange silence there, with no one around not, even a crow.
"It's emptier than, it used to be..."
"Yeah, I think nowadays kids spent more time with phones and games, they have no time to play at this fun place..."
"They are seriously missing a lot...!"

"Shall we have some fun?"

"Why not...!"

"What are you guys doing here?" asked Riya. Shreya, Maya, and she, all came to find out the boys. They were bathing cum playing there, in their boxers. They got shocked and jumped, and started trying to hide using anything they could get their hands on. Girls couldn't help but started laughing immensely until their eyes got teary.

"What are you doing here?" asked Mayank, hiding behind his shirt, not too successfully I must add.

"We were looking for you guys, when we couldn't find you at school; we knew you guys would be here..."

"We came here to bath; there is a long queue at school..." said Shreya, while Maya was hiding behind Riya.

"Just wait outside!"

"Fine, finish fast...!"

"Just go!" both boys said in a sharp screaming voice.

Chapter - 11

"You dance well...!"

"Really?"
"Yeah!" said Maya to Ravi. They all were dancing in the auditorium, DJ was full-on Masti and the volume was on full, you could hear it in the toilets near, too. Maya was dancing with Ravi while Shreya was with Mayank, and Riya was standing and drinking alone near the food counter, pretending to enjoy them.

"Who is that girl?"
"What? Where..."
"There...! Near the gate behind DJ..."
"Where? I don't see anyone..."
"She is standing right there, look...!" said Maya pointing in that direction.
"Are you making fun of me, there is no one?"
"No silly, I am not, she is right there..."

"Where, why can't I see?"
"She is wearing a school dress, clean but old... The one we used to wear during our school days..."
"Seriously, I can't see anyone..."
"Okay, leave..."
"What are you doing?"
"Dancing, what else do you think?"
"It does not look like dancing, seriously"
"Why...? I always dance like this...!" said Mayank to Shreya.
"You are just jumping strangely..."
"No, you are slow...don't blame me...!"
"Who is that boy, behind you?"
"Where... I can't see anyone?" she said turning behind.
"Behind you, near the entry gate, about 12 or 13 I think in school dress like we used to wear".
"Don't mock me..." she said and pressed his foot by her heel.
"Ouch… I am not!"
"He was there, just a minute ago..." he said looking here and there.
"There is no one..."
"Okay... okay, maybe it was my imagination..."

The dance happened till 10 pm after there was dinner. Then our gang left to go out for drinks, they returned at around 12:30 am. Drunk they all were but still in consciousness, Riya was on Maya's shoulder, Ravi was being dragged by Mayank and Shreya was behind them singing something with heels in her hands.

"Guys, you heard something..."

"Not now, we are exhausted and I will sleep right here...if you disturb our walking again...!" said Ravi, who was not exactly walking.

"Shhh… listen!" said Shreya and put her finger on her lips.

"Everybody, just stop!!!" she said this time screaming. Everybody stopped.

"WHAT…!"
"Can't you hear someone laughing?"
"Where... I can't!"
"Shhh, I heard something too..." said Maya.
"It's laughing...but not of one person's, it's multiple people..."
"Yeah, I heard it too..."

"But where is it coming from...!"
"It seems... everywhere but how!"
"Guys let's go...walk faster, I am having a bad feeling..."
"You always have a bad feeling Maya, just listen carefully..."

"What do you want to listen to, it's a laugh, not a standup comedy...!" said Riya to Shreya.
"Yeah, she is right. Let's just leave..." said Mayank, now you could see the fear on his face.
"It's midnight; I don't think we should follow some laugh".

"Yeah! let's find out...! Who is laughing at this time..." said Ravi drunk, trying to leave Mayank's grip.
"Just stay here and shut up...!"

"Let's go, now..." he said forcing. Everyone walked fast and went straight back to school, this time from the front gate. They were too distracted to think about it.
"Shit…!"
"What...!"

"We forgot to come from the back...!, There will be a guard running towards us, anytime now..."

"Shh… keep your voice down, let's just walk fast and go inside, before anyone sees us..."
"Fast with this..."

"Okay… just walk quietly..." said Shreya, they walked very quietly if you consider kicking soda can quiet, or falling after every sound came. But for their advantage, there was no guard there. They went to bed and passed out.

"Wake up, it's morning...!" said Riya and Maya, trying to wake up Shreya. "Just a couple more minutes and don't shout my head hurts..." she said pushing them away. They had been trying to wake her up for the past half an hour, without any progress. On the other hand, Ravi was doing some exercise on the ground, at the back of the school. Mayank had gone to bring some breakfast and something to make them lucid.

Chapter - 12

"Here take it..." said Mayank, handing over coffee to everyone.
"Just this...!"
"No, omelette and toast are coming with some orange juice, anything else you would like, Mam...!"
"Okay... okay don't be sarcastic like my sasu maa..." Shreya said to him.
"You are married, you never told us...!"
"You bitch!!"
"What…! When?"
"Shut up, I am just kidding..."
"Ohhh..." said everyone in unison.
"Guys, do you remember about last night...!"
"What is there to remember?"
"Aree…! That strange laugh, we all heard..."
"There was probably nothing, we all were just drunk..."
"No, I can bet. I heard it...!"
"So, what about it..."

"Who do you think was laughing in the middle of the night?"

"How would we know...?" said Maya, sipping from the cup. "It was probably our delusion..."

"I swear to God, I heard something..." said Shreya, blowing air in the cup.

"What about that girl, at DJ...!"

"What girl?"

"I saw a girl behind DJ while we were dancing... I told Ravi, but he says he didn't see anything...!"

"Yeah... because I didn't, I am saying truth...!"

"There was not a girl but a boy near the entry gate... I saw him and told Mayank, but same... he saw nothing!"

"No, I saw something..."

"What… why did you lie then?"

"I saw an elephant cycling and juggling with his trunk...!" said Mayank and both of them laughed while Shreya got annoyed.

"Let's see the school if we could find our old seats or not..."

"What, yaar Shreya just sit and drink...!"

"Just come with me, it will be fun..."

"Okay, I am coming and.... what about you Riya?"

"Fine, I will come too but only if Ravi comes..."

"Why are you dragging me into this?"

"Just come, na…!"

"Fine, let's go...!"

Chapter - 13

"Look, there is our class...!"
"Yeah, we can see Shreya..."
"You are never excited about anything..."
"What do you want... should I jump in excitement?"
"Whatever…" she said annoyingly. They went inside and it was the same as they left it, well not exactly, there was not the regular black board with chalk and duster placed down at its right corner. Instead, there was a big screen, for the smart class and a projector too, back in the classroom. The seats were now looking new.
"Damn…! They got everything replaced..."
"So, what would they suppose to do instead...? Shreya!"
"Yeah, I know it's been a decade but yaar, Maya…"
"Guys look, come here...!"
"What is it, this time...? Ravi!"
"Look, the seats are the same just painted..."
"Yeah, I can see some leftover of our names, on the top..."
"Wait…! Let me clear it..."

"What are you doing...? What if anybody sees us...!"
"There is no one, Maya... chill!"
"But why are you scratching it with your keys, Mayank...!"
"Look, now it's clear, you can see Shreya and Riya written on it, by compass..."
"Yeah, so many memories, right Riya...!"
"Yeah, I remember the day we engraved it..."
"It was after school... I think...!"
"Yeah, after everyone left..."
"Why aren't our names here?"
"Why we would have written...your name? Ravi!"
"Because we are friends...!"
"Like you wrote our names, at yours...!"
"Point taken!"
"See here is ours, 'Maya and Ravi'...!"
"Yeah, we wrote it during the class..." he said and laughed. "Not we, you...!" said Maya. "Okay...Okay, I did..." Then they went to Mayank's classroom, even when he insisted not to.

Mayank's classroom was next to theirs after the water machine in between. It was also a replica of other classrooms, that's how schools are designed. But, Mayank was not happy like them, after seeing his old class; he was running away from all those memories, which still haunt him sometime in dreams. Now he was standing right in front of those memories and he just froze. In his eyes, were going on the flashbacks of what happened there.

"Hey, what happened Mayank...! Where are you...?"
"Huh… nothing, just let's leave!"

"But why...? You haven't even shown us your desk yet...!"

"I am leaving; you guys stay if you want to..." he said and left in a hurry, they all followed him.
"What happened bro?"
"Nothing!!"
"Come on, Mayank... tell us!"
"I don't want to Shreya, just leave me alone for a while..."
"We are not going anywhere until you tell us..."
"Just go...leave me alone!"

"We are not," she said and they all stood there, silently. He just stood there silently looking down from the railing and for a while, he didn't utter a word. They also didn't say anything to him.

"You guys won't leave me alone...!"
"NO, we won't...!"
"Fine, I will leave..."
"You are not going anywhere, too," she said and grabbed his hand to stop him. "I told you, it's nothing let me go..." he said and left.
"What is wrong with him?"
"I don't know... Riya I don't know!"

Chapter - 14

"I always wanted to see this place, it's quite nice..."
"Yeah, we were not allowed to come here, during our school days..."
"One time I even tried to sneak in, but got caught...!"
"Now that we are here, the view is very good..." said Ravi, standing and stretching his body. They were sitting on the school's roof, drinking beer. The cold breeze was flowing, touching their cheeks and playing with girls' hair.
"Look guys, come take a look...!" said Shreya looking down from the roof.
"What is there?" said everyone and looked down.
"Yeah, that's what I am saying...there's nothing...!"
"You stupid!" Riya said and hit her.
"But there's something, there...look someone is walking there..."
"Where...? I don't see anyone...!"
"There... look!" Maya said pointing towards something, down there.

"Yeah, she is right, someone is down there"
"But who is walking, at this time...!"
"He looks like a kid, doesn't he?"
"Yeah, but it is not a He, it's a She...!" said Maya.
"No, it's a boy...!" said Ravi.
"He looks like a boy, you are right..."
"But She's a girl..." said Riya, scratching her head.
"Let's go down to help him, maybe he's lost..."
"Are you out of your mind...? I am not going down...!"
"But, what if he's lost...!"
"I am not going...!"
"We are not even sure... if it's a boy or girl...!"
"We will see. When we get there..."
"No means no, we are not going down there.... are you insane it is night time. It's not a good decision!"
"Maybe it's a ghost; let's meet him or her, whoever it is...!"
"I am ready...!" said Ravi.
"I am not going...!" said Maya, scared.

"I am not going there, at any cost...!" said Riya. They dragged her with them anyway, as they reached down, there was no one. They looked around a bit but couldn't find anyone.
"See no one here...! You were worried without any reason..."
"But why is the air got cold suddenly...?" said Riya shivering while rubbing her hands. "Yeah! the temperature has gone down, it seems...!" said Maya and Shreya. Soon they all were shivering and rubbing their hands.

"I have heard that it gets cold when there is a ghost nearby..."
"Don't scare us, Shreya...!"

"Yeah, shut up!!"
"Why...? Ohhh... there is a ghost...! He will catch us...!" said Ravi, spooking.
"Stop it… Ravi!"
"Yeah, let's go back, I am sleepy..."
"Okay! Okay! fine!"

"WHAT THE FUCK!!!!!" said Mayank, and screamed.
"Huttt….hutttt….dooor huttt…" Ravi was shouting. It was a black dog that came out of nowhere and was barking at them.
"It's just a dog, guys...!"

"It's not a dog...!" said Ravi, pointing in its direction. It was as black as night and bigger than normal. It had sharp pointed teeth and it was breathing heavily, you could see air coming out of his mouth because of the cold. His feet were as big as a human hand, and strangely it had no tail. Eyes yellow with a hint of red in them. He was barking at them but stopped when they noticed and started gazing at them. There was something different in those eyes, as horrified as they were, they were like trying to tell something. He could have jumped at them, but it looked like, he just wanted them to leave.

They ran, as he barked again. Ran with all their might towards school, went straight into beds, and said nothing.

Chapter - 15

"What the hell was that?"
"Don't ask me...!"
"I am going home, right away...!"
"What… why?"
"What do you mean why...? Didn't you see what happened last night!"
"But the Reunion is still on...!"
"So what...! I don't want to die because of a fucking reunion...!"
"Yeah me too! I am packing..."
"I have already packed last night; I am leaving as soon as possible..."

"What are you guys doing...?" said Shreya, they all were sitting in the classroom, after the incident they all were pretty terrified. Some of them even wanted to leave but they can't because the school was on lockdown, as the very security guard of the school was missing. The rumors were spreading like fire, some were saying that he was drunk and ran away, some said he stole something from school and fled, some said he was the child kidnapper who is pretty famous nowadays, on TV.

"Don't go, we should stay..."
"But why?"
"Because this is our school and we owe it to it. We have to keep it safe...!"
"We have our lives too...!"
"Wait a minute... guys! So that's why the guard wasn't there the other day..."
"So what?"
"So he is the son of Mansukh Uncle, remember him?"
"Yeah, he was the guard, back in our days..."
"Yeah, I remember too, he was always nice to us kids. Such a nice soul he was...!"
"Yeah, I heard he died a couple of years back..."
"Ohh...! He's his son...!"
"So what...? Maybe he's the kidnapper, or maybe one of the other rumors is true..."
"You can't be that mean, Riya..."
"Yeah she is right...!" said Shreya.
"No, it's no way right..." said Maya, insisting.
"I am staying...!"
"Yeah, Mayank is right, me too..."
"Me too...! What about you...?"
"No, I am going as soon as the lockdown gets over...!"
"You want to stay... so stay! I am coming with you Riya..." said Shreya, they both were leaving; others were going to stay.

Chapter - 16

"So what's the plan now?" asked Ravi. They all were sitting at the tea joint, now there were only three of them left. They decided to start searching from the security guard's house. They enquired about his address from the principal, even after he declined to give them that at first, they made him do it. He said them not to put their nose in this matter, they had already informed the police, and the investigation was on. They still left and went to his house, as they got there, the police were already there, so they waited for them to leave.

"Let's go, the police's gone..."
"Wait, what are we going to ask them?" asked Maya.
"Just come, we will see..."
"Hello, Is this Sandeep Bhai's home...?"

"Yeah, but who are you?" asked a lady, opening the door. She looked like his wife, in middle age, and wearing a saree and sindoor.

"We are Sandeep Bhai's friends; we came here to meet you...!"
"Meet us, why?"
"We know he's missing, and we are here to help..."
"What are you going to do? Police had already asked us questions..."

"We won't bother you much, just a couple of questions..."
"No, sorry I can't let you in; I don't know any of you...!"
"Please, let us help; we used to go to the school, where he works...!" said Maya, insisting. She was doing the talking, you know women to women. She didn't let them in but they were still insisting, when an old lady came from inside, she was the widow of Mansukh Uncle.

"Who is here, Sangeeta?"
"No one mummy Ji... just some people, they say they know your son!"
"Who are you?" she asked coming from behind.
"Aunty, it's us! You remember us?"
"Who are you?" she said, putting her glasses on.

"Aunty, we used to go to the school... where your husband used to work... try to remember! You have met us while we were kids. You once came to school for the Diwali celebration to decorate the school and we helped you.
"No, I don't remember..."
"Here, look at this...!" said Ravi swiping on his phone's screen.

"Yeah...now I remember you kids! But why are you here today?"

"We have come to help... to find Sandeep Bhai!"

"Let them in, Sangeeta..." she said going back inside; she was older now, much older. She used to be pretty, but then it has been ten years, she had to grow old. Her black hair had turned gray now with some still black ones left, her saree was old too, looked like being worn for a long time. She wasn't wearing her gold mangal sutra, which she used to wear back then. Her husband loved her very much, and Sandeep was her only kid. After her husband's loss, she had lost her charm.

Chapter - 17

"So tell me... when you last saw him...?" asked Ravi, they were sitting which was the only room in the house, sipping tea. She told him that she had last seen him two days ago when he left for work but he didn't return home that day and has been missing since. They asked her about Mansukh Uncle too and told them how sorry they were, to hear about his death.

They asked his wife too if, he was worried about something or had trouble with anyone recently. If he had told her about any problems at work or someone had been troubling him. She told them that he, once said, that he had seen some things at school, some unnatural things like ghosts. Though she didn't believe him then, now she was worried that something bad might have happened to him. They didn't tell her about their encounter with the supernatural; instead, they consoled her and left.

"So, what now?"
"Now we go back to the school, where he was last seen...!"
"Let's go, then..."

AT SCHOOL

"So, you met him on that day, when he went missing...?"
"Yeah, he came to meet me that day. He told me that he hadn't slept well for the past couple of days..."
"But why?"

"Because one day... when he was on duty after school, he heard something! And followed the sound. He saw a girl sitting in an empty classroom, weeping. He went inside to see if she still hadn't left school, but when he touched her shoulder, he got shocked out of terror and lost consciousness.
"But what did he see, exactly...?"
"He told me that, he saw..." he said, gulped, and shifted a little from his place. Then told them that he saw the girl didn't have a girl's face, instead, it had a face of a boy.
"What…! How?"
"I don't know, that's all he told me..."

"Okay thanks for your help, we will leave now...!" said Ravi, they were asking questions from a peon of school. They asked questions from as many as they could. Staff also told them that they had heard some noises too, but never saw anything.
"So what now, we have asked everybody...!" said Mayank.
"I don't know! I am not a detective..."
"Neither I am...!" said Maya.

"So what! We just wasted our time...we should have left with Shreya and Riya...!"
"No, we did the right thing...!"
"Yeah, Mayank... he is right!"
"We should check the school's record register... to see if anyone else has taken any leave recently."
"But why?"

"Because something had happened and somebody knows about it too, who stopped Sandeep to go deep into this matter. Maybe he started looking about that girl or boy and he found something, something worthy of not let be shared with anyone. We have to find out if someone else has left his place and has gone on leave recently because he or she will try to hide for a while. If they have kidnapped him he should be with them.

"Yeah... maybe you are right. Let's find out...!"
"But how? Principal won't let us touch records, because police would have told him to do so..."

"We will sneak in the record room, quietly at night!"
"But the reunion is over; he won't let us stay at school anymore...."

"We have to ask him, to let us stay...!"
"What do you want, exactly?" said the principal in surprise.
"We want to stay at school for a couple of days, till the investigation finishes..."

"But it could take months, I can't let you stay here. If something happens... I will be held responsible!"

"No sir, we will take full responsibility for ourselves!"

"NO, I said clearly! You can't stay here..."

Chapter - 18

It w "We can live here, for a couple of days..." said Ravi; they all were in a room, at a hotel nearby. They booked two rooms one for Maya, and the other for boys but they all were in the boy's room, planning what to do next. They left the school instantly after the principal told them.

"If any of you want to go, you still can..." said Maya, sitting on a chair at the corner of the room, while Ravi and Mayank were on the sofa.
"No, I don't want to...!"
"Me neither..."

"Okay... we have to get the records somehow, now it's harder than before..."
"Yeah, but how? Now we have to get into school..."
"We could sneak into the school, at night...!"
"No way, I am not going there at night time...!"
"But we have to..."

"Yeah, he is right, Maya. We don't have a choice..."
"Okay, I will go..."
"Let's go tonight...!"
"Tonight!!!!" said Maya
"Yeah, the sooner the better..."
"Okay, Ravi and I will go inside, while you watch outside..."
"So this is it, guys...! We are here. Now as planned we will go and Mayank, you stay here...!"
"Got it, go...!"

"Come Maya," said Ravi and they went inside by climbing over the door. The school was empty and nothing was there but darkness. Inside was all black; they had never seen the school this empty. The record room was on the third floor at the end of the corridor. They had no trouble going up and finding the room, it was written over its entrance gate. But it was bigger than they expected, there were three lines of iron shelves with three shelves in each line, full of papers and files.

"Let's start... you search on the first shelf. I will get the second..."

They searched all the shelves but couldn't find the records, they were looking for. They were just leaving when something strange happened; a file fell from one of the shelves. It was the record of 2012, two years after they left. It was not the record of leaves or attendances; there were other documents in it, like testimonies of people and stamp papers.

"What is it...?" said Maya, showing the file to Ravi.

"Looks like a file of court documents..."
"Inside it has some papers...I am trying to read, but they are too old..."
"Keep trying...!"
"What… what was that?" said Maya, surprised. They heard a loud sound like something heavy fell.

Chapter - 19

"Where are you, Ravi?" said Maya, screaming. They left the class immediately after they heard the sound, tried to follow it but somehow in the dark Ravi and Maya got separated. She was trying to find him but he was not on the third floor and the third-floor door got locked, so she couldn't leave. She tried multiple times but it seemed like the door was locked from the outside. "Shit! Stupid gate...!" she said and kicked it. "Where the hell are you? Ravi...!"

"Where the hell, I am...?" said Ravi, looking for a way out. He was inside, what looked like a darkroom, though it was all dark still, he could feel things, like some old seats and tables. It felt like a storage room, full of old-school materials. He couldn't see his hand, it was so dark and his phone suddenly stopped working. He tried knocking and shouting but there was no one outside to hear his voice. On the other hand was Maya, trying to find him and failing miserably but somehow she opened the door.

"What the hell are they doing inside... why it's taking so long?" said Mayank, worried and waiting for them outside the school. The air was so cold and it was freezing outside, he was shivering even after wearing a lot of warm clothes. He wanted to drink hot tea and be in bed under a warm blanket just being cozy and all warm but instead, he was on road in the freezing temperature. They all were stuck under different, strange, and unfavorable circumstances.

Chapter - 20

She was still not being able to leave school because Ravi was still nowhere to be found. She checked all the classrooms on the second floor too, but he was not there too. She went further looking for him and saw a shadow hiding behind a door, though she was scared like hell, she still went to look at it. As she was getting near her heart started beating faster, she was sweating like she just completed a marathon. With every step forward her feet were getting heavy and harder to move but she still gathered all her courage and decided to open the door.

Mayank was still sitting outside; shivering but now he had another problem. Police were on patrolling rounds, if they saw him, then it was over for them. He hid behind a car and prayed that no one come outside of the police car. But to his bad luck, the car stopped and a constable came out with a flashlight. For a moment, his heart was beating faster than the F1 race car, or at least he thought that. Constable was getting near him, he tried to move back but hit a wall, with no way to go, it was just a car between him and jail.,

Ravi was still locked in that room, and now he was bleeding too. He cut his hand, trying to open the door; somehow he managed to stop the bleeding by wrapping a piece of his t-shirt around his hand. He stopped trying and was sitting on the floor when he saw two eyes looking at him from the end of the room. For a moment his heart stopped I think, but he managed to stay in his senses. They were human eyes but there was no one just two eyes staring at him from the darkness. He tried to move but couldn't move his body, he tried to scream but no sound came out of his mouth.

As she opened the door she was relieved, it was nothing but a shadow of a tree. She went closer to the window to see outside, the air was flowing and leaves were dancing in it, she looked outside right and then left but saw nothing, it was too dark. Something jumped on her and she screamed so loud it echoed in the whole school. She fell and dropped her phone, she tried to search for it but its flashlight was no longer on and it was too dark for her to see, she then looked ahead to see what had jumped on her. It was a cat, who in front of her eyes turned into a kid with a black body and glowing eyes, walking on all four, coming towards her. She managed to get up and ran out of the room with all her might but it caught her leg and dragged her inside, she screamed as the door got closed.

Ravi heard her first scream and started shouting "Maya… Maya….Maya! Are you there?" "Are you alright...? What's happening...!", but heard nothing back, the two eyes were still looking at him. He wasn't able to move or talk as you know already, so the above scene of him shouting only happened in his mind. He was still sitting in the same position as those two eyes came closer to him, he wanted to run but his body didn't. From the darkness emerged a black kid, walking on hands and feet; same as in Maya's room but the kid came close to him and stared right into his eyes. Ravi could hear him breathing and could feel his breath on his face, the thing opened his mouth and, a red tongue came out, long and swinging. It licked Ravi's face and he could feel the coldness of the tongue and wetness of saliva, it licked his face all over, as he closed his eyes out of fear.

Mayank was getting hyper as the constable was coming close and close to him, he hid the best way he could, as the flashlight touched his face. It was over he got caught and because of him, his friends would get caught too. He still turned out to be useless as he was in childhood but for a twist, only light touched his face before the constable could see him he heard a scream of a girl from inside the school, panicked and ran back to the car. He took a breath of relief as he saw the police car leaving, but the scream was definitely Maya's. He tried calling both of them but couldn't reach them; so he decided to go in, himself. As he was about to go in, a car came, so fast out of nowhere, didn't even give him time to react, and stopped just before 1 inch of his right foot, as he fell.

Maya kicked whatever the thing it was, opened the door, and ran full of her might towards the school's exit door but couldn't reach it, because she was somehow teleported to the record room once again. The file they saw earlier, came flying in her face, she caught it and without wasting another minute ran towards the ground floor. She was finally able to go out of the school building, she was expecting Mayank to be waiting for them but there was someone else too.

Ravi was finally able to get control over his body, punched the thing in the face, and ran. He met Maya, on the way but they didn't stop and kept running until they were out of the door.
"What the Fuck!!!"

"Don't be scared, it's us...!" said someone coming out of the car, the headlights were still on, though he couldn't see any face the voice sounded familiar.
"Who are you?"
"It's us!" said Shreya, finally visible as the lights turned off, there was Riya too.

"What…! What are you both doing here?" asked Mayank in a surprised tone. Right then Maya came running out of the door, followed by Ravi both panting and wet in sweat.

"What happened to you guys?" asked Shreya, holding Maya and Riya helping her.

"Yeah, I heard a scream. I tried to call but couldn't reach any of you, what happened inside...?"

"Just leave... let's leave from here!" said Ravi, panting and running towards the car. They all followed and left to the hotel, got another double room for the newly arrived. That night nobody talked neither Ravi nor Maya, they were too stunned to speak, and they just passed out on the bed. Ravi and Mayank already had a room together, and Maya slept with Riya and Shreya, she was too scared to sleep alone. In the middle of the night, both Maya and Ravi woke up, a couple of times, maybe because of a nightmare or something.

Chapter - 21

"So are you sane enough to talk about last night?" asked Shreya to both of them. They all were having breakfast in the boys' room, so they could talk, for a couple of minutes, there was only silence, different from the one when they first met at the reunion. This silence had fear and terror in it.

"First you tell, what happened...! Why did you both come back?" asked Mayank, as both Maya and Ravi were still afraid to speak.

"We left as you guys saw but in the midway, my car broke down and while I was waiting for a lift, I stopped Riya's car. She was coming back because she didn't feel right about leaving you guys behind, so I sat in her car and we came back. "Why did you leave then?"

"Let's leave that topic and focus on the hot potato here"
"What happened with you guys, last night?" asked Shreya,

as her words reached their ears, the flashback started in their minds.

"Hey… are you alright?" asked Riya touching Maya's hand. They told them what happened with them last night, as shocked as were others to hear them, they also were shocked hearing each other's stories. Again there was a silence and again different from both last times. This silence had a void in it, which could suck all of them inside. The silence wasn't caused by fear or awkwardness, it was caused because nobody could figure out what to say.

"Guys... I am so scared right now! What should we do now...?"
"Me too, I think we should all leave..."
"No we can't, we have to solve this case...!"
"Come on, Ravi... you almost died last night! You still want to continue this?"
"Yeah... as we have come past, the point of no return. Whatever it is... now we are a part of it, we have to continue. What you say, Maya...?"
"Huh… what?"
"I asked what you think about staying or leaving...!"
"I don't know, exactly..."

"Take some rest, we will meet later this afternoon...!" said Shreya and they left Maya alone to sleep; Ravi was not in the mood of resting. He went out for a walk, alone. Shreya and Riya went out to meet somebody.

While walking, Ravi got near a park, where they used to play as kids. As he sat on the bench there, he went back in time as a kid. He got up from the bench as a kid in school uniform, his friends were waiting for him to play hide and seek. It was Mayank's turn to find them, as he started counting, they all got hidden; Mayank completed and walked further to find them. He saw what he thought was Ravi, hidden behind the water fountain; he slowly walked ahead as he reached his hand to touch Ravi. It was not Ravi, it was a dead body hidden behind the fountain.

He screamed and ran, everybody came out of hiding and everyone else at the park also ran towards him. When they all saw a dead body, they got shocked, the police came and told them that it was a body of a boy from the nearby area. That was the day they all first time saw a dead body, they went straight home that day and took a couple of days off from school, afterward. They wanted to go to school but their parents didn't let them when they came back to school there were rumors at school. Rumors were that the kid got stuck in some gang war and got shot at; others said that he was doing drugs and another druggie killed him in a fight.

The rumors were high but no way near reality, the reality was that the kid got kidnapped and when his family failed to pay the ransom, they killed him and threw his body at the park. The bark of a dog brought him into today once again, he was thinking about that incident, maybe it was something bigger than just a mere kidnapping, maybe it's somehow related to the recent disappearance of Sandeep Bhai and Ghostly encounters.

Chapter - 22

Maya was in deep sleep when she had a dream of the same incident that Ravi remembered at the park. Riya and Shreya were looking for someone who could help them in reading those documents, which were in the school's record room. They met a lawyer, who told them that it was a case file in which a student in the year 2000 filed a report against the school, which said that the school was somchow involved in child disappearances that happened at that time. But nothing could be proved and the case was closed. Other documents were of some property case suits filed against the school.

"So, what you think?" asked Riya, they were in an auto, going back to the hotel.

"I don't know anything now... something big and bad is going on for quite a while low. Now the time has come to put it to an end...!."

"I think we should tell others to leave and go home..."
"But they won't...!"
"Maybe now they would, after the incident at school..."
"Let's see what Maya has to say in it, she would have gotten up by now..."

They guessed right, when they reached, Maya was already up and Ravi was also back. They were waiting for them to return. They told them about what the lawyer had told them and Ravi reminded them of that incident that happened years ago. Somehow, though nobody knew how it all feels connected, that Murder, those cases, and the recent ghostly encounter accompanied by another disappearance.

"So what do we do now?"
"I think we should go into school again, to see if we could find some records of that student who filed the case...!"
"What was the name of that student again?"
"The report says 'Manisha Roy'...!"
"Manisha… never heard of her!"
"How could you...? She was in school ten years before us..."
"Yeah... another decade of mystery! It's been twenty years now..."

"Hell! I am not going into that place again...!" said Maya. "Me too!" Ravi accompanied her. "But we have to; it's the only way to find out and solve this mystery..." said Shreya. Then again the room went silent for a minute until two people agreed to go, and those were 'Shreya and Riya'". But this time they were trying to break into the school, at day time, which was risky because now they have to worry about living people and hope so not about dead ones.

This time they went into school by pretending to be teachers, as the school was closed for police investigation, and there was no one, just a new security guard. Placed by the school management, who was also afraid to go inside, and he didn't know about the staff there, they just fooled him into thinking they were teachers, who had some papers inside they needed to collect. He would have called someone from school management to ask about them, if Mayank hadn't given him Rs.500 and insisted, that they had to complete their work earlier but they didn't, and if he reports, they all will get into trouble, so don't. He let them in finally, after a couple of monetary conversations.

After that, it was easy just to go inside and on the third floor; both Shreya and Riya were inside, trying to find something that would help them. It was a beautiful day, nothing to be fearful of; they were searching free-minded and were indulged deeply in the pile of files and papers. After a couple of hours, they couldn't find anything regarding that case.

"There's nothing here...!" said Riya, throwing away a file.
"Yeah, I don't think we would find anything useful here..."
"So what now?"

"I don't know..." Shreya said and sat back lying on a shelf, as she laid back the shelf moved a little and a file fell on her. "What the hell is this?" said Riya rubbing her head. "It's a file!", "Look!" she said surprisingly looking at the file. It was the file they were looking for. They felt someone was looking at them from the room on the opposite side of the corridor.

"Who is it?"
"How would I know?"
"Let's go...we should check, Riya..."
"No way, let's go back...!"
"I think we should check...!" said Shreya, she wasn't scared but intimidated to find out about that thing.

Chapter - 23

"So what did you guys find?" asked Ravi, as they were sitting in the hotel room.

"We found this...!" said Riya, showing them the file. "What is it?" asked Ravi turning the file up and down, left and right. "It's the record file, about that case filed by Manisha Roy. In that file, were papers regarding the case of children disappearances, seven children disappeared at that time and neither any evidence nor the children were found. Due to lack of evidence the case got closed.

"We should go and ask the parents of missing children. Maybe we would find something useful..."
"But how we gonna find them...?"
"Here is a list of addresses of those children...!"
"Great, we should start from tomorrow then..."
"Ravi is right, we should talk to them..."
"Yeah, there are seven places. We should divide...!"

"Yeah, you two go at these, and we three will visit these..." said Riya pointing towards the list, it was divided into 3 addresses for each group and the last one they would visit together. They went to a restaurant that night, they all were scared and stressed, and a couple of drinks could definitely help in making things better.

The restaurant was good with decent lighting and good furniture, the crowd was much but not that much. They were sitting at the middle table at the right corner of the restaurant, waiting for the order to arrive.

"How strange it is, isn't it that we were at that school for years, going every day through those doors and corridors but, never saw or heard about these events. Never even saw a ghost there, even when we tried to!" said Ravi jokingly and laughed.

"Yeah, I remember when we tried to find a ghost but couldn't find anything..."
"Yeah and see now, it's all over the news. The world knows about it now...!"
"Never thought in my life, that I would see this one day..."
"Me neither..."
"Maybe it's still not, maybe it's all just a big conspiracy...!"
"No way...! It's fake I know what I saw that night at school..." said Maya, hesitatingly.
"Yeah, I will never forget that night, it was the most horrifying night of my life...!" said Ravi and gulped.
"I am sure... you both are saying the truth but, still there could

be something humanely in this and not supernatural..."
"We never thought that one day we would be sitting in a restaurant together and talking about something like this...! At least I didn't!"
"I did remember our school days and all of you, on a couple of occasions...!"
"I missed you guys too... I did!"
"We all did...!" said Ravi.
"So... how come we never met, even once in these past years...?" asked Riya.
"So much had happened, we just got lost in our lives..."
"Yeah... I had thought about a meeting like this, where we all meet and remember our childhood days..."

"At that age, I never thought we would get so strange to each other. But here we are now, sitting in a restaurant talking about a case we had nothing to do with, a couple of days back. Now it's all that interests us...!"
"You are right, Mayank...!"

"So... set aside this thing for a while and tell me how are you guys, really doing?"

"As we told on the first day. Just usual day to day life..." replied Shreya.

"Don't give me that bullshit; there has never been anything usual with us. Just tell... I think we should talk because if something has bound to happen with us, we should clear the air between us...!"

"Nothing is going to happen to us...!" said Riya mockingly. "You don't know that, I mean these two almost died that day... One day maybe we would...!"

"He's right... I am down to talk, what about you?" said Ravi looking at Maya.

Chapter - 24

"Can you tell me, where this address is?" asked Ravi to a man, showing him his phone. He told them that this address had changed and if they want to know they have to ask Mr. Mukesh, who was the oldest living resident there, he would probably know where it is. They went to his house and rang the bell "Ding…Dong….!" A sound echoed inside the house and an old man in his sixties maybe, opened the door. He called them inside and made them sit in the hall, while he made tea for them. The house was old and had that smell which comes from old books; there was no picture on the walls simple plain blue colored walls with only one picture of a lady, maybe his late wife.

"You wanted to know some address right?" he asked sitting on the chair in front of them with a cup in his hand.

"Yeah, this one!"
"Let me see...!" he took the phone in his hand and put on his

glasses, which he moved up and down a couple of times to look at the screen.

"Do you know where it is?" asked Riya, trying to look at the phone's screen. She came with him, while Maya, Mayank, and Shreya went together.

"Hmm…" he hummed while rubbing his chin. "Yeah, I know it. Wait a minute!" he said and went into a room, bringing back a diary in which multiple addresses and phone numbers were written. He told them that the house is nearby, just in the second lane. Asked them too, why they want to go there, they told him that they are their relatives.

"I think we are lost!" said Shreya, they were trying to find their addresses and everything was changed in past years, people living there were new and didn't know anyone. They were flats and nobody knew who lives next door, nor do they care.

"I think we should ask someone!"
"Don't need to Maya, I have it under control..."
"Yeah, as you said 10 minutes ago...!"
"Don't give me sarcasm, Shreya..."
"Quiet! Both of you... and focus on the task..."
"Okay, let me ask someone..."
"Fine, go ask...!"

They finally found the address, but it took them another half an hour. It was a decent small house, there was everything except happiness, a strange vibe of sadness was there like happiness resided at this place at some point but had left long ago and forgot to return.

"So who are you and why have you come?" asked a lady, while they were sitting, she let them in because they said they know something about their children disappearance. First, she said no then they told her Manisha's name and she agreed.

"As we told you, we are here to talk about your son..."
"What is there to talk about, it's been ten years. Nothing left to talk...!"
"We are investigating the disappearances that happened at that time...!"
"Investigating? Who are you, police?"
"No we are …." Maya was about to say something but Shreya interrupted.
"We are Private Investigators, investing disappearance of Sandeep Ahuja. A person recently went missing from the same school, your kid used to go to..."
"Okay, what happened?"
"We don't know, that's what we are trying to find, mam..."
"And we need your help for that...!" said Mayank from behind, while the girls were doing talking.
"What do you want me to do?"
"Just tell us, exactly what happened...!"
"Though it happened ten years ago, the memories are still fresh..."

TEN YEARS AGO

"Ma, I am back. Where are you?"
"In here!" she replied from the kitchen and the cooker whistled.

"Give me something to eat, I am hungry...!" he said while sitting on the sofa, throwing his school bag on the floor. He loosened his tie and removed it, opening the upper button of his shirt. He was what you say a normal teenager, just reached a height of 5'10 in last summer vacations, thin but not weak with a little stubble on his chin and under his nose.
"Gaurav, how many times I have told you not to leave your shoes here".
"Hmm…maybe a million times!" he said and laughed.
"Shut up and put them in place...!"
"Okay will do, first give me something to eat..."
"No, first put them in place and go put on some clothes. Put your school dress in the washing machine..."
"No, first give me something to eat naa… I am hungry!"
"I will give you nothing until you do as I say...!"
"Okay, I will do it!" he said and got up from the sofa. Did everything his mother told him. After that, he ate and went to his room, in the evening he was watching TV while his mother was cutting vegetables for dinner. He sat near him and told her...
"Ma... I think someone was following, coming home from school..."

"What… who?" she said, instantly stopping her hand and giving him, her full attention.
"Nothing…! I think it was just my imagination..." he replied and went back to TV.
"Stop watching TV. and come here...!"
"Let me watch, Ma...!"

"I said, come here. Now!" she said in an angry voice.
"Okay," he said, sat there, and told her that maybe someone has been following him for a couple of days. She instantly calls his father told him everything.

The next day his father went to drop him at school and also talked to his school's principal. The principal told him that he will tell the security guard to keep watch, in the meanwhile, he could drop Gaurav off at school to make sure about his security. That day he came back and kept dropping Gaurav for maybe a month. It went on for a while, he still felt someone was behind him and one day he was gone. No sign, just gone and never got found. Police investigated the case but the trail went cold, and he never came.

"He never came back, I kept waiting for him but he didn't...!" she completed her story, tears had started to fall on her cheeks. Girls instantly moved near her to console her.

"So, what did the police say about it?"
"Nothing…they just closed the case!" she said sobbing. "So how do you about Manisha?" she asked, wiping tears.
"We know that she filed a case against the school..."

"So you would also know that we lost. That innocent, sweet girl went bitch, somehow and refused to be a witness from our side, and because of lack of evidence, we lost.

"But why, why did she do that?"

"She didn't tell anyone... and soon her family left this place and sold their house...!"

Chapter - 25

"We want to talk about your daughter..." said Ravi, they finally got the right house, it was a two-bedroom flat maybe. Not too shiny but with dull lighting, there was no joy in the air, just emptiness. They were sitting on chairs with her father and mother; they were a middle-aged married couple, with no hint of happiness on their faces.

"Why do you want to talk about her?"

"We are working on a case that might help us know, what exactly happened to your daughter...!" said Riya.

"There is no point in talking now...!" said the girl's father, angrily.

"Please listen, we need your help. Your help will probably save a life."

"Who's life?"

"There is a man that has gone missing and we think his disappearance might have something to do with your daughter's"

"But how? It happened a decade ago. How it could be connected?"

"Because I think, maybe the same people are involved in this too."
"And who are you?"
"We are helping police in the investigation..." said Ravi, while Riya stared at him like an eagle.
"Nowadays... police take help from immature people!"
"No sir... we are professional. We often help police in insider investigation!" Ravi said again, Riya coughed.
"Okay, what do you want to know?" asked Aravi's mom.

"Mam, tell us exactly what happened...at that time!"

She told them, she used to drop Aravi at school. But for a couple of days, she got busy with some work and couldn't drop her. She started going with her friends, one day she came home scared and sweating. When she asked her what happened, Aravi told her that someone was following her on her way back home. We got scared and the next day I and her father went to talk to the principal, he told us that he has already told the guard to be more careful and immediately inform us if he sees anyone following the kids. He also has informed the police regarding this.

One day when she was coming back from school, this time with her mother. Someone followed them, when they turned back there was no one, so they kept walking until someone hit her mother on the head and took Aravi. When she regained consciousness, she was nowhere to be found, police couldn't find anything and the case went cold.

"So there were no clues, nothing at all...?" asked Ravi.
"No, the police told us they found nothing, no fingerprint, no footprint, no CCTV footage," replied her mother, now sobbing.

"We lost our precious daughter and nobody did anything," said her father, trying to control his tears.

"Did she tell anything specific to you, like who was following her, or was it just her or her friends too...?"

"No, she told nothing special. It happened too fast, we couldn't do anything..." said her father. "I wish we had stopped her from going to school that day," said her mother. "Sometimes at night, I think if I had not lost consciousness, she would be with us now...". "Sometimes I pray to god, they would have taken me instead," now her mother was crying and her husband was consoling her.

"I am sorry, please stay strong...!"
"Yeah we couldn't take away your pain, but we could share it..."
"We will find what happened to her..."
"We have lost all hope in the past ten years!" said both of the parents.
"We will try our best, we should leave now. Thank you for helping us...!"

Chapter - 26

"So, what did you guys find?" asked Mayank, they were sitting in their hotel rooms.

"Just that, the kids got abducted on their way back from school," said Ravi.

"Yeah, two were abducted when they were alone. The other two were with their parents when they got abducted..."

"Our two got kidnapped on their way to school, early morning...!"

"So, all kids were kidnapped either going to school or coming back from school. It means the school has something to do in this matter...!" said Riya.

"Yeah, something bad was going on at school, at that time..."
"But how do we find out, exactly what happened...!"

"That...I don't know," said Shreya.

"Maybe we should ask the police, about what they found," said Maya.

"Yeah, and get caught for using their name. Very good idea" said Riya in sarcasm.

"So, you tell us then, what to do...?"
"Don't you two, start fighting...!"
"Let's eat something first, I am starving!"

"Yeah, Ravi is right, we will think about it tomorrow. I am very tired and starving..."

"Let's go to the restaurant!"

"No, I don't want to. Let's order something!" said Mayank, lying down on the bed.

"Okay fine, let's order..."
"What do you guys want, I am giving the order...?" said Riya holding the phone in her hand.

The next morning they went to ask people if they know about Manisha's whereabouts but nobody knew where she and her family went. They didn't tell anybody. The gang found an address of a relative of theirs, still living in the area. They straight went to their house to ask but, there was no one they were looking for. The house had been sold to a new family, who had no idea where they went.

"So, we are back to zero, then...?" said Shreya, frustratingly.
"Yeah, I think so, you are right..."
"What do we do now?" asked Maya
"We could go back, and forget about it like it never happened...!"

"Again you came back to leave. If you want to go, then go, I will stay!" said Mayank to Riya.
"I am also staying, I've never done something worthy in my life and for the first time, I feel like I am doing something important. That I am more than a fucking accountant...!" said Ravi, he was furious.
"Yeah, Ravi is right. What we are doing is important!"
"Yeah, I know it's important Shreya, but it's not our work to do..."

"So, then who will give justice to those kids, if not us. It looks like everybody else has already given up on this...!"
"Yeah, like you are a very noble person, na...! Shreya. Like you always were the star kid of the school, everybody's favorite!"
"What are you talking about, Riya. You too were just like me; at least I didn't leave you in the middle as you did..."
"Hey…hey easy guys, please don't fight!" said Ravi.
"Who left you, I never left you alone...!"
"As you did, when I needed you and just like that, you were gone!"

"What!… when did that happen...? I don't remember it?" said Maya, and Mayank followed her.
"There was a reason! And when you don't know something... don't blame someone!"

"What…what was the reason? Tell me! Why didn't you tell me earlier?" "Let me tell you why because there was no reason... you just got bored with me and you left...!"
"You don't know anything... don't you shout at me!" said Riya furiously and now her eyes started getting wet.
"So go on, tell me. What was the reason?"
"Just leave it. I don't want to..."
"No, don't leave! I want to know the truth...!"
"I think, you should settle this, it's been too long," said Maya, holding Riya's hand.
"No, I don't want to!" she said and shook her hand.
"See... now she is backing off because there is no reason. I knew it!"
"Yeah, you are right! Okay... just leave it!" said Riya now crying.
"Don't start crying, we won't get infected by your tears. Tell us, we all want to know."
"Why don't you tell us, what have you been doing these days. I know you don't work at a fashion magazine, so don't lie to us...!" Riya said trying to get ahold of her.
"Wha…what?" said Shreya in a shocking tone.
"Yeah tell us... why you lied to us?"
"I don't…. I didn't…. lie. I said the truth!"
"See there... she is lying again!" said Riya pointing towards Shreya.

"Don't you dare! Call me a liar... You Bitch! You betray people..."
"Shut up, I too can raise my voice. And don't abuse, you lying bitch!"
"Yeah, I lied, so what...!" Shreya shouted in anger.
"You did what?" said everyone except Riya.
"Yeah… I lied, so what. Don't make it a big issue...!"
"But why did you lie?"
"Because I wanted to!"
"But why?"
"Because..." she said and paused.
"Yeah, why?"
"Yeah, tell us, Shreya... why?"
"First you tell us...!"
"No you do, yours more recent matter. Mine's too old!"
"So what...! Old means it doesn't matter, anymore?"

"Please, guys stop fighting...!!!" shouted Maya, so loud that even people nearby started looking at them, and the gang was shocked that, Maya could scream like that. She always had been a silent one.

Chapter - 27

"I lied because… because I lost my job!"

"What… what happened?" asked Ravi going near her but still maintaining a safe distance.

"Because…." She said and sat on the ground crying, Maya also started crying while Riya was already in thc mood. Only the boys were dry. She told them that her boyfriend died in a car crash, in which she was driving. She told them, how many times she wished, it should have been her who died. She lost her senses and went crazy, made a scene at the company, and got fired. All the pain she tried burying in her was now on the surface like oil on water. She told them how she started drinking and lost control of her life, shifted to a different place. So many sleepless nights of crying and regretting, how they shouldn't have gone on a drive that day, or how they should have taken a cab. She was crying like heavy rain.

"I am so sorry to hear that, Shreya," said Maya.
"Me too..."
"Me too, Shreya," said Mayank and sat beside her.

"I am sorry, I didn't know that happened. I just wanted to blame you for something; I didn't mean to hurt you. I am sorry Shreya!" said Riya, who now had stopped crying and had sat near Shreya, putting Shreya's head on her shoulder. She was still sobbing, didn't say a word to anybody, they all hugged her. Left and went back to the hotel that night girls slept with Shreya and she still didn't say a word. She didn't eat either, it felt like she was lost in her mind, probably didn't even notice when they brought her back to the hotel.

"So what's your reason?"
"Haaa…! What?" said Riya, she was scrolling on her phone.
"I asked what your reason was. I mean we heard Shreya's... but, why did you lie!" asked Maya.
"I… I didn't lie, who told you I lied...?"
"I know you don't work at an MNC, there is no point in lying!" Maya said looking straight into her eyes like she could see her soul.
"Wha… how do you know and since when?" she asked in awe.
"I knew from the beginning..."
"How? And why didn't you tell anyone?"
"I didn't want to embarrass you, so I kept my silence!" "So, why did you. Tell me!" said Maya.

"First you tell me... how you know?" she asked, thinking

maybe Maya don't know the whole truth and she could still lie somehow.

"One day I came to meet you at your old resident, but I found out you don't live there anymore, in fact, you haven't lived there for a very long time..."

"Why did you come to meet me?"

"I wanted to talk to you about something..."

"About what?" she asked to divert the conversation.

"Nothing important, you tell me now...!"

"Okay fine!" she said, took a deep breath, and told her everything. First Maya was in shock, then she felt sorry for her and hugged her. She went through so much alone, for a moment Maya forgot her worries.

"Why didn't you call me? I would have come to help you...!"

"I just didn't want to, I wanted to live alone. I didn't have it in me to face any of you!" Riya said with teary eyes.

"Okay... don't worry it will all be fine. Now you are better... right?"

"Yeah, you could say that," she said now crying.

"Don't worry I am here with you, we all are" Maya said wiping off her tears. Riya hugged her tight and cried; she was filled with pain but couldn't tell anyone. When she told her, she felt a burden off of her shoulders. She just let her pain flow away in tears, emptied herself.

"I think you should tell Shreya, she would understand and will forgive!" Maya said with an innocent face like a cute teddy.

"I don't know, how to...!" she replied.

"I will help you, don't worry," Maya said and put her to sleep.

Chapter - 28

"So, how's she?" asked Ravi.
"She's fine, asleep though..." replied Maya.
"And how are you, Riya!" asked Mayank, coming from behind, yawning, and stretching his arms.
"I am good, thanks for asking!"
"You two made quite a scene yesterday. I am worried about Shreya..."
"Yeah Ravi, me too!"

"She didn't say a word the whole night, just kept sobbing 'as I could hear her crying'. Then, sometime at night, she fell asleep..." said Maya. They all were sitting outside the hotel in "what I think was a garden once, but now was converted into an outside restaurant".

"I had no idea; she was in so much pain. I mean she showed no signs, since the day we met, she was fine to seem!"

"Yeah, she seemed fine to me. Even under the influence of alcohol, she didn't break. Which indicates consumption of alcohol regularly...!"

"What about you Riya. What secret...do you hold?" asked Ravi, looking at Maya.
"I am not holding any secret. What do you mean?" said Riya.
"I mean, Shreya was asking... why you left her!"
"Nothing..." Riya said and looked away.
"Come on, tell us. What is it with you and her, when exactly you left her?" "As far as I can recall, you were always with us".

"I can assure you, there is nothing for you to worry about!" said Riya, frustratingly.
"Easy Riya, Ravi is just asking...!"
"He should mind his own business!"
"But...this is my business, I work for the gang...!" Ravi said and laughed.
"Shut up…!!"
"Just tell us, naa…!" said Mayank.
"If I wanted to tell you, I would have by now!"
"So, why don't you want to?"
"Because it's a matter between Shreya and Me, we will resolve the issue. Don't interfere!"
"We just wanted to know, I never thought, you two had a secret relationship behind our backs...!"
"There was no relationship. Just shut up!" Riya screamed and put her cup on the table and left furiously.
"What is wrong with her...?"

"Yeah, what's her problem...?" asked Mayank after Ravi.
"Nothing, she's just tensed about tomorrow. She just needs to resolve her issue with Shreya, then she will be just fine...!"
"We could only hope!" said Mayank and Ravi.
"Let's go, we should check on Shreya...I am sure she must be hungry too...!"
"Yeah, let's go"

They went to Shreya's room; she was curled up on her bed like a little snail, with a phone in her hand. She was so lost in her thoughts, that she didn't even notice when they came into the room. They didn't say anything just stood there, silently.

"Should we say something" whispered Mayank in Ravi's ear.
"I don't know, what you say, Maya?"
"I think we should leave and come back!"
"Why are you all whispering?" "I can hear you!" said Shreya, still curled up. They moved a little close to see if it was her who was talking, or they all were hearing voices. Ravi went a little too close almost fell on Shreya, but got saved by Maya.
"You are up, we thought you were sleeping...!"
"Yeah, it's fine we could come back!"
"No...it's fine!" said Shreya, getting comfortable and wiping off her tears.
"We just came...to check on you!"
"Thanks, I am fine!"
"Okay, that's great. We will come back later!" said Ravi, trying to leave.
"Wait a minute! Would you like to eat something? Let's go grab a bite! You must be hungry" said Maya and stopped Ravi by grabbing his shirt.

Chapter - 29

"I think we should ask principal sir about this... maybe he knows something...!"
"What do you think he will tell us Riya? If he had anything to do with it, he will decline, and if he hadn't then he will strictly tell us to leave. He had already told us once before!"
"Yeah, Mayank is right!"
"I think we should go back to school and try to contact the spirits; maybe they would tell us something."
"Are you nuts!" said Ravi, after he spat a fountain of water while drinking.
"I mean why not, maybe they will help us."
"Yeah, you are saying this Shreya because you weren't there when we almost died of a heart attack!" said Ravi in a repulsive tone.
"Ravi is right; no way, I am going back there. Not at any cost!"
"I can't think of anything else..." said Shreya.
"So what?"

"Well, I think, Shreya is right?" "There is nothing else we can do now"
"So Mayank, you and Shreya go there, I am not going."
"Okay, I will go and you Mayank?"
"I will come too...! I couldn't think of any other way to continue this investigation!"
"So, it's final, tomorrow we will go. Let's see what happens!"
"Fine with me!" said Ravi.
"Let's go tonight!" said Riya, everyone looked at her like she was about to reveal the new 'I phone'.
"Are you okay? Riya" asked Maya.
"Yeah, I am fine. I will go with them!"
"But why do you want to go? That is not a place for tourists...!"
"Because Ravi...we have to keep going on, and now we are stuck. We need to do this!"
"I know why she wants to go because she is ashamed of what she did to Shreya, and now she wants to look good...!"
"Ravi, shut up! That's not the point here..."
"But why are you suddenly so helpful, as I recall you wanted to give up till yesterday and now you are ready to put your life in danger."
"Okay guys, don't fight, if she wants to go, let her..." said Maya, stopping them from creating chaos.
"You stay quiet Maya, who do you think you are, our teacher, who will say something and we all will listen!"
"I didn't mean that, I…"
"Since you have arrived, you act as our leader. Who made you a leader?"
"What leader? Riya...! Where is this coming from?"
"Riya is right... you had always been like this like, you are our

mother and we have to behave in front of you...!"
"Shut up, please don't talk to me like that!" said Maya on the verge of crying.
"Go back to your sweet husband if you don't like our way of talking....here we talk like this!" said Shreya.
"Guys please, stop don't do this to her. She meant no disrespect to anyone...!"
"Shut up Mayank! Don't interfere between us...!"
"I am not interfering Riya...I am just saying…!"
"Yeah, he is just saying because now he is successful and rich... so we were supposed to listen to him!"
"What rich? Ravi, I was just trying to calm them. Why are you putting this on me?"
"Because you think... you are more successful than any of us, so we would listen to you. Let me tell you...nobody ever listened to you, and nobody will!"
"Yeah, like we don't know... how big of a loser you were in school. Yeah, don't be surprised! We knew but never told you anything!"
"Ho….How do you know about this?"
"We all knew! Just because you were in a different section doesn't mean we couldn't have known. We heard your class students talking!"
"So why didn't any of you... say something?"
"Because we didn't want to hurt your feelings."
"I never told you... because I was embarrassed and scared... that you all will leave me too!"

"We never would have done that...! If you just had said something... we would have helped you...! But instead, we had to pretend like we knew nothing!" said Riya.

"Sorry guys…I am so sorry!" Mayank said, now with tears in his eyes. He never thought that one day; his friends would say this to him. He always thought that, when he will tell them, they all will hear him and understand him. Now the situation was the exact opposite, they all were blaming him for not telling them. Even in his worst nightmares, he wouldn't have thought of this happening.

"Keep your sorry to yourself... we don't need it!"
"Why are you guys fighting, first Maya and then me? "What is happening here?"
"Nothing is happening, we are just showing mirror... to the two of you!" said Shreya.
"Ravi say something and Maya please stop crying yaar…!"
"What do you want me to say, Mayank!"
"Anything... just stop them...!"
"I don't care; let them do whatever they want...! For 10 years...! You all were like didn't even exist, and suddenly everyone cares about each other's lives!"
"So what, it's not like you called us every year to wish... 'Happy Birthday!'"
"Why would I... Riya? You could have done this!" "And Shreya... you too!"
"Yeah, so I didn't call any of you. So what?" "Did anyone ask me how I am? 'No', you just cared what I do!"
"It's not like you asked any of us, yourself...!"
"Shutttttttt Upppppppp……!!!" screamed Maya, louder than she did before. Everyone went silent, looking at each other

and not knowing what to do. They had pressed some buttons, they shouldn't have, not knowing what to do or how to react, everyone just left the room one by one.

Chapter - 30

So, as you all know, our guys had a big fight and they weren't talking to each other. For a while, I will tell you guys what happened next, as they had planned Shreya, Riya and Mayank went to school the next night, yeah "Night!", you heard correct. While Maya and Ravi, stayed back at the hotel, not sleeping but worried, they didn't want to show but they care deeply about them, after all, that's what friends are for. Maya was praying for their safety while Ravi was pretending to watch a movie on TV, but his mind was at school.

They entered the school, as expected there was no one to keep a watch. They smoothly went inside from the backside through 'Old Valley'. Let me tell you, they should have gone by the front gate, what they were about to witness will change their lives forever. An event they will never forget, it's going to play a crucial role in the further investigation as well as will decide what will happen to their friendship?

All three of them were inside the school now, not in the building but the boundary walls. For their bad luck, they chose a new moon night, without the light of the torch; they couldn't see their hand in front of their faces. They thought there would be some kind of lighting inside the school or at nearby places but as they put foot inside the school, everything around the next three blocks went black, it was a blackout. They could hear the dog crying far away but still audible. Shivers went down to their spines; they felt cold more than they should be. The wind was chilly and it was making strange sounds by flowing through leaves and branches. The rustling of leaves and the sound of their hearts were adding more fear to the scene.

They still weren't talking to each other, normally, just only when it was extremely needed. With every foot forward, their fear increased. They all wanted to hold hands but nobody said anything, the gurgling sounds of their stomachs were the only sound coming out of their bodies, except their heartbeat. Slowly they moved forward in a group close to each other but not too close.

"What the fuck was that?" said Shreya breaking the ice; something ran from behind them extremely fast.

"How the hell would I know?" replied Riya, breathing heavily.

"I told you... we shouldn't have come!"

"You did? When? You wanted to come too!"

"Yeah, whatever!"

"Shh… listen, you heard that. Someone is crying!" said Mayank, signaling them to be quiet.

"Who the hell is crying at this time?" asked Shreya looking here and there with a flashlight.

"Let's go, I don't feel good here," said Riya. They reached inside the school building as expected there was a total blackout. With lights in their hands and fear in their hearts they walked further down the corridor. The crying was still audible in the background, though nobody was visible. But they had come to ask for help from ghosts, so they have to talk to them, there was no point in being scared. It was colder inside as compared to the outside. Now it was showtime, no more hiding they have to come in the middle and talk to them. "Hello… Mr. Bhoot, how are you?"

"What the fuck! Are you here to ask for help, or to invite them for a tea party!" Shreya said annoyingly to Mayank, who was scared but still trying his best to act like he wasn't.

"I am just trying to be nice!"
"They are dead, not sad... you duffer!"
"So, you talk Ms. Ghost communicator...!
"

"Fine!"… "Hello, we are here to help; we want to know what happened with you. Help us so we could help you...!"…. "If anybody is here, please... we come in peace. Don't hurt us... we just want to help!" said Shreya, looking around and scared that someone might actually show up.

"I think it was not a good idea, we should leave!" said Riya, praying that nobody shows up.

"We can't, we are past the point of no return!"
"Who said that? We could still go back...!"
"Let me try again...!"

"No... this time, I will do!" said Riya stopping Mayank. "Hello, is anyone here? We want to know.... what happened to you! See we cannot help you until we know exactly what happened. This time something happened, the crying in the background suddenly stopped. A sheer terror went down to everyone's spine still, no one was in sight but, even in this cold they all were sweating, which was making them colder when the wind touches their sweat every time their heart pounds.

Chapter - 31

"We have to meet Mansukh uncle's wife once again... I think she knows something. She hadn't told us!"

"Yeah, Riya is right. Let's go for a meeting..." said Shreya; they all were at the restaurant having dinner.

"She definitely knows something...!" said Riya.

"Don't talk like that! We are still not sure if she has something to do with it!"

"You don't know Ravi... what we saw yesterday. That's why you are saying this!"

"Riya is right, I will never forget that night. It's still going on in front of my eyes!" said Mayank and drank some water.

"So, then let's go tomorrow...!"

"Yeah... and I am sorry Maya for what I said that day!" said Ravi.

"I am sorry too, please forgive me!" said Shreya.

"Me too, I shouldn't have said that to you Mayank. Please forgive me..." said Riya, folding her hands in a praying gesture.

"I am sorry, too Mayank. Sorry, buddy!" said Ravi and patted Mayank on the shoulder.

"It's all right, I forgive you all..." said Mayank.
"Me too!" said Maya.
"So, we're fine?"
"Yeah, we are fine!"
"So much has happened that we didn't know about each other. Still, we said those things..."
"Yeah, I feel so bad..."
"Don't worry Ravi, we are fine!"
"By the way, I did beat Suraj's ass one day!"
"What…when?"

"You remember...! When he slapped you without any reason. I saw it from the corridor, I was out to drink water later that day I beat his ass and told him not to touch you again!"

"Ohh…! So it was you! I wondered for so long what caused that change of heart in him. But it worked he never said anything or touched me again..."

"Yeah, you should have seen him. He was like don't beat me, Mummy…mummyyy…bachaooo…., though I only slapped him, Once!" said Ravi and they all laughed, after a long time together.

"Hello is anybody home?" asked Ravi knocking on the door.
"You people again! Why?" asked Sandeep bhai's wife, opening the door.
"Is aunty home? We want to talk to her!" said Shreya from behind.
"Yeah she's home but why?"
"Can you please call her?"
"Maa…..!" she screamed inside.
"What is it, why are you screaming? I was sleeping..." said aunty coming from behind.
"They have come again to meet you...!"
"Why are you here today...? Did you find something about my son?"
"Yeah aunty, we want to talk... in that matter!"
"So tell me what did you find?"
"Aunty it would be better if we talk inside!"
"But why? Tell me here!"
"It's a serious issue; we want to talk in private!"
"Okay fine, come!" she said and moved inside.
"Sangeeta, put on some tea..."

"So tell me, what you want to say?" she asked sitting on the floor in front of them.

"Aunt…aunty, we want…to say..." said Shreya, she always had liked her and never in her wildest dream would have thought that, one day she would have to say something like this to her.

"We have found that.... you know something about a cult that used to sacrifice kids in the 2000s..."

"Wha...what are you saying? Are you out of your mind! I know nothing about any cult or whatever!", she said straight to their faces without a hint of guilt in her eyes. "What proof do you have against this claim?" she asked getting slightly furious.

"You want proof, we have proof!"
"Wh…what proof do you have?" she said, now with a little fear in her eyes.
"We know that Sandeep Bhai... was a member of that cult! Who used to sacrifice kids!"
"What... I know nothing about it. I would have to say you... to leave my house!"
"And I would insist you sit, or we will go to the police. We have proof...!" said Riya. "We know that Sandeep Bhai used to murder innocent kids from our very school!."
"Don't talk crap about my son! He did nothing of that sort...!" she said furious in a voice loud enough that Sangeeta heard it and came.

"There is no point in raising your voice. We have proof that the cult used to kidnap and murder kids, brutally... We think that Sandeep got afraid that he might get caught as we saw things, the first day we came to school and he knew we would look into this, so he ran away. We don't think it was a disappearance, we think it was a dangerous criminal running away from the police!"

"Shut up…!!" she said and the room went silent. Again silence, it seemed silence was now more popular than voice. This time this silence had anger and fear, and guilt in it.

"He was innocent, he did nothing wrong. It was his father!" she said and started crying, Sangeeta sat near her to console her.

"What…!!!" said all five of them.

"Yeah, it was him. He was the member of the cult called 'Araogan Satan'" she said wiping her tears from her saree's corner.

"Shit… I never thought something like this would be the truth!" said Ravi sitting down on the floor.

"Yeah man, I still cannot believe that Mansukh Uncle was involved in something like this. He was so sweet with us; he was such a nice man. He never even got angry on a kid, ever...!" said Mayank putting his hand on hand.

"You got it wrong, it was not Sandeep...!"

"Well… for that. We had no idea about who was involved, we just knew about killings and a cult..." said Maya.

"Wha…what, but you said…!"

"Yeah, we lied! To make you tell the truth... We knew Sandeep Bhai was innocent and also your only son, so you would never let someone blame an act like this on him, a hideous crime!"

"My son was innocent and he didn't even know about this side of his father. He always thought of him as a normal school security guard, an innocent, kind-hearted man!"

"We too thought about him, like that!", "But, how…and why?" said Ravi and Shreya.
"It's a long story, it happened years ago…"

Chapter - 32

20 years back…

"Sandeep ke papa, where do you go these days... late at night?"
"Nowhere, why you asked?"
"I have seen you, sneaking out at night and coming back late..." I asked, swinging the fan with one hand. He was eating lunch and I was sitting next to him, he had come home at break time from school.
"I go out with some friends, nothing more," he said and drank water.

"Ohh... okay!" I said. Though I was still suspicious that something was going on behind my back but I said nothing more because I also didn't him to get worried.

Later that night, I followed him when he sneaked out of the house. The clock was striking 1'o clock at night; the wind was sweet as it was a summer night. I maintained a safe distance from him, so he wouldn't detect anything. He crossed the house street then the main one. Went to the main road then behind the old water tank, and then into the closed office of the water station. I stood near the office gate, trying to hear the conversation going on inside. I heard some talking but couldn't understand a word, it sounded like a strange language.

I felt like a meeting was going inside, there were a lot of different people's voices coming from inside, and waited until the meeting got over. An hour or so passed, when he came outside and went straight back home; I took a shortcut and reached home before him. He came and slept beside me I was pretending to sleep.

The next day he went to school as usual for work, I didn't mention anything about what she saw last night. Last night was hard for her; as a result, she didn't sleep well and messed up his morning tea, so he was already annoyed. It was good not to say anything then.

I didn't say anything too when I went to school to give him his lunchbox which he had forgotten. He did notice something strange in my behavior though I think but said nothing because he was afraid that I might have suspected something. Things went back to normal for a couple of days since he stopped going out at night, until one night. He sneaked again but I woke up when he smashed his leg into the table accidentally. He was standing in front of the school talking to some people. He went into school this time, I followed him. I hid behind a wall to see what was happening; there were seven or eight people maybe, all in black robes with hoods. They all were chanting something in a strange language, then they went inside the canteen and brought back something with them, it was dark, so I couldn't see anything. It was a man, a real human with his hands tied at his back and a mask over his face. He was so much alive and resisting but looked also badly beaten up and with a slap from that man, he fell and they laid him in the middle and formed a circle around him. He looked like he had passed out but still breathing heavily in the silence of the night you could hear his breathing behind the chants.

Then one of them brought a big knife and opened his face, he was unconscious but they brought him back with a sprinkle of water. It was clear that they were going to kill him but that too with him being known, what was happening to him. He tried to scream but his mouth was covered with a cloth. He kicked, head-butted but couldn't get out of their grasp, then they made something on his head with a red powder and Bam!!!! They chopped his head off, I almost screamed seeing this hideous scenario but silenced myself, and then I passed out.

When I woke up, I could see the fan on the ceiling, rotating. It was my own house; I soon realized and instantly woke up and sat straight, to my surprise my husband was also there, sleeping next to me. He too woke up sensing that I was up, I got scared and moved a little away from him. He came near me and said "Don't be afraid, I am not going to harm you!", then he gave me something to drink, at first I hesitated but then drank it. After that something strange happened it was like I could see things that weren't there, not even in the same realm. I saw fire, a lot of it, a place that looked like Hell, scary creatures eating dead human flesh and torturing the live ones. Then I saw a long line of people shackled in chains, going inside the mouth of a big horrifying creature, it closed the mouth after they went in and I could hear their screams and the sound of their bones being shattered and crunched. Then she saw two big thrones on them were sitting, what seemed to look like humans, but definitely weren't because the horrific creatures were obeying their commands and were scared of them, too. They were like some high authority ones, who looked like humans except their eyes were the exact opposite of us, they had black eyeballs and white Iris.

Then she saw some other humans being skinned, some others being thrown into the river of blood and something else, by the cliff of a mountain. Then came a big throne, bigger than the other ones, with spikes behind it and it was standing of skulls and bodies of humans, some of which were still with flesh. On it was sitting someone far scarier than anything she had seen yet, someone that was the face of terror, in his eyes were eyeballs made up of blood, his face was something you can't describe. As he turned her face towards her, it was like he could see her, he opened his mouth, and inside were tormented souls, screaming. She immediately woke up, still able to hear the screams and faces moving in front of her eyes but this time she was in her home, that she was sure of.

She was all sweating and breathing heavily, he gave her a glass of water then he told her that what she saw was 'Hell' and Satan himself, on the big throne. He went inside and brought a pendant with him, told her to hold it, and as soon as she did, all her fear was gone she was calm as a goat. She asked what it was and what was happening, he replied that they are bringing Satan into the human world. There is a book called 'Omayun', an ancient book that was written by a person who once almost called 'Satan' on earth, but some people got him and killed him before he could finish the ritual.

They had found that book and were trying to do it successfully, what he couldn't. 'But why?' I asked, and then he said that he is the real God, the one who will give them, eternal life and all the prosperity there is to get. I rebelled that this is wrong, and he had gone mad, doing horrific crimes but then he gave me the pendant, again. It had a star on it, with some names written in each sector of the star. Names of Satan, different names according to different cultures and periods, the pendant was of pure gold and he told him that it was a gift from the Real God himself.

She asked what he was going to do, "It would be better if you don't know", he said. Then she didn't ask any further questions and they never talked about it ever again. She knew it was wrong and a crime but somehow she also wanted to get rid of this poor life, she had always dreamed of a good life, but never got it as her father was also a poor farmer, she spent her childhood in hunger and thirst, then she got married and moved to the city but it was still the same life, one room in the slums and a long waterline. She didn't agree with him on his face but also said nothing and kept her silent.

Chapter - 33

"Holy shit!" said Ravi and Mayank.

"Oh my god!!" said Maya.
"What the fuck!!" it was Shreya and Riya. These were their reactions after hearing the horrific true story and reality of who they thought was a sweet and kind person, Mansukh Uncle.

"That's the whole truth, I told you... My son had nothing to do with this, he is innocent!" she said, now Sangeeta was not consoling her, she was in deep shock and couldn't figure out I guess, how to react.

"Yeah, but who knows, if she is telling the truth or not, or maybe Sandeep was too involved in this, after all, he was their only son!" said Riya.

"No!!... I told you he was not involved in anything!"
"Yeah, if you say so!"

"Keep it together, Riya!" "Can you show us the pendant and the book... Do you still have them?" inquired Mayank.

"No, I never saw the book in real but, I still have that pendant... somewhere!"

"Can you show it to us?"
"Wait…I will be back!" she went inside and brought back a pendant, nothing like anything they had ever seen.

"It's cool and amazing!" said Ravi, taking it in his hands.

"It looks like gold but definitely... does not feel like it!" said Shreya, rubbing her fingers on it.

"Let me see...!" said Riya, and looked at it from both sides. "Yeah, it definitely.... is not gold. At least it doesn't feel like it...!"

"It's cold, though it was inside a trunk with clothes on it. It's so cold like it was placed outside in this cold temperature!" Mayank said. The markings on it were like engraved in it. The names were still visible, though they were in some foreign language, a strange one. It was twenty years old but still shining and hasn't lost its color like it didn't oxidize. Maya said clearly "No" to touch it. She even told them not to touch, who knows what that thing was, definitely not from this planet.

"We are going to keep it...!" said Shreya.
"What… why?" everyone reacted in shock.

"We might need it, in the further... investigation!"
"Yeah, I think you are right!"
"No way! We are keeping that thing... with us!"
"Don't worry Maya... it's just a pendant. I will keep it...!" said Riya.

"Can we?" asked Ravi to Aunty.
"Keep it! I don't want that thing in my house, maybe my son is paying for our bad deeds... it's karma striking back!"
"You should have thought that, before!" said Riya in a sarcastic tone. She was still crying buckets of loads, but this time her daughter-in-law was nowhere near her, she was still thinking or maybe she went numb.
"Please, find my husband...!" she finally spoke; her tears were shining in the light.
"We will try our best, don't worry!" said Shreya, holding her hand, then hugged her.
"That was a lot to take in, guys...!" said Ravi, driving. They were in his car going back to the hotel.

"I never could have imagined something, this evil...! Behind that sweet and caring smile..." said Maya. "You can't judge people of how they look or act. Now I got it, why do people say that...!"

"Yeah, Shreya is right. I would have believed for one time that Sandeep was behind all this but never Mansukh uncle!"

"He was surely so much more... than a mere security guard!"
"It's just half the truth, guys. We still haven't found anything

about the cult, God knows... what truths going to reveal in this investigation..."

"First you move your ass...! That's the truth we all know!" said Riya to Shreya.

"Where to… the car ends here, see!"

"I told you to get two cars...!" Riya said to Ravi, but he ignored or maybe he was in deep thoughts. Well, though their backs were hurting, something was hurting, even more, their broken trust.

Chapter - 34

"I think we should look out for that book. What was its name?" asked Shreya, they were sitting at the cafeteria of the hotel.

"I think it was 'Omaku'"
"No, Ravi, I think it was 'Onamu'"
"No, it was definitely 'Oamapu'"
"Shut up, all of you, it was 'Omayun'" said Riya.
"Yeah, that one!" said Mayank in agreement.
"How would we find anything about it…? There's nothing on the internet related to this name..."
"I think we should ask, Shrekant sir. He might know something about it."
"Who is that?" asked Ravi.
"Stupid... our librarian!" said Shreya.
"Ohh, yeah I remember!"

"No, you don't...! Because you didn't even know that we had

a library at school," said Maya, and they laughed together after a long time.

"That's not true, I knew it. Okay!"

"Okay…okay fine!" said Riya, still laughing. Mayank almost fell off his chair.

"So, where is he now... anybody knows his whereabouts?"

"No idea, man...!"

"I think we should go into school again... maybe we would find something about his old address!"

"No... Not school, again…!"

"Yeah, Maya is right. We don't have any other choice!"

"Fine...but this time, we'll all go, okay?"

"I think that would be best... if we all stay together!" said Maya.

"Yeah, this way if one of us dies or only one of us stays alive, he or she could tell everyone, what happened to the rest of us. More people mean more chances, right?" said Ravi, jokingly.

"Shut up!... Nothing is going to happen to us but still it's a good idea to go together...!"

"Let's go tonight!" said Mayank.

"At night… Are you mad? We would go in the daytime...!"

"No Riya, it would be better if we go at night because we can't go inside at daytime!"

"But why?"

"I saw a police vehicle outside the school, so I inquired and found out that police was now going to put up security outside the school...!" said Mayank.

"Why?" asked Shreya.

"Because they found out someone has messed up the files in the record room. It means someone had broken in...!"

"So, we got caught?" asked Maya.
"No, we are fine...! They didn't even try to find out who did that, they just increased security!"
"Good... so how can we still go at night?" asked Ravi.
"I don't think so... the constables will dare to stay there at night and even if they did, we could sneak in while they doze off!"
"Yeah, Mayank is right. So, tonight it is...!"
"Yeah, the sooner the better..." said Riya.
"Let's get done with it...!" said Maya, they all were scared but nobody told anyone that. Nobody even detected. I think as you grow old you get better at hiding your fear or your emotions behind a fake face.

"Excuse me guys, I have to make a call...!" said Ravi, and left. They went inside to do their things. They had nothing to do; Mayank went for a walk alone. Shreya again was looking at her late boyfriend's picture and crying. Riya was thinking about her mother. Maya was missing her husband. They all were sad but didn't say a word to each other, they got very good at living alone, or they forgot what it feels like to have someone who cares and loves you without any judgment.

"Hey, can I sit here?" asked Riya, pointing at the bed where Shreya was sitting.
"Hmm…"
"How are you?"
"Why are you asking this?" she asked looking up at her from the phone.
"Just asking, as a friend..."

"I am fine...", she said with a straight face and turned her gaze again to the phone's screen.

"Okay... good…" she said and went silent for a minute. "You know, why I did? What I did...!" She said in a slow voice looking down.

"Wh…what?"

"I never betrayed you; I never wanted to leave you alone, but…"

"Okay fine... I heard it. Now please leave me alone...!"

"Please listen to me for a minute. I want to tell you the truth...!"

"What truth?"

"Why I left you...!"

"I don't want to hear....it's been so long. Forget it...! I have...!"

"No, you haven't...I know! Don't lie to me; I know you still want to know the truth...!"

"Yeah, you know everything, right...!"

"Don't get angry, I don't want to fight. I just want to talk to my old friend. I want to talk to my, Sheu!!"

"You remember it!" Shreya said, now finally looking up at her.

"Of course! Why wouldn't I?... I was the one who gave you this name!"

"Why did you... leave me, then?" "You know, how lonely I felt and how strange.... being with all of you all day at school, thinking what I did wrong that you left me and not being able to know that. I used to think where our friendship went wrong, was it something I did or just you got bored..."

"You didn't do anything wrong and I never got bored of you...!"

"So why… Tell me!!"

"I…" she said and took a deep breath her eyes got a little teary.

"I thought you would not like to hang out with me, anymore..."

"But why...!"

"Because my father's business went downhill and we lost everything. We always were princesses of our fathers, daughters of businessmen, but when my father lost everything, I thought we wouldn't connect anymore, because I lost the thing we had in common!", she said in one breath.

"What!!!... I didn't know that. When the hell did that happen?"

"It started when we were in tenth, but I didn't tell anyone, I was afraid of how you all will react..."

"You should have told us or at least me... I would have been still your friend... doesn't matter if you have money or not. That was not the only thing we had in common... we like the same stuff...same cuisines... etc., that was the base of our friendship and we understood each other, better than anyone!"

"I just couldn't... I am sorry!" she said and cried.

"Don't cry. I forgive you… Come here, you stupid girl!" she said and hugged her.

"I am sorry…" she kept saying in her arms.

"I am sorry too... I should have understood, I was your friend but I didn't even ask. I should have...!"

"No, it's not your mistake. It was all me!"

"No, it was mine too...!"

"You both had your part in this... It was a joint mistake!" came a voice from behind the door, it was Maya.
"She is right; we both did our part in this."

"Come here!" said Riya and the three of them hugged together.

The friends were back, at least some of them, others will come soon too. I know friends can't lie to each other for long and they definitely can't keep secrets from each other.
"If both of you are done crying, can we go and eat?... I am starving!"

"Yeah, let's go!" said Riya and Shreya, wiping off their tears. Mayank was back from his walk, by that time. He joined them too, and Ravi came along.
"So, we are on tonight?" asked Ravi.
"Yeah, we are ready!" said both Shreya and Riya in unison.
"That's something… you two used to sound like that at school time...!" said Mayank.
"Yeah, because we are going to school again, right!" Riya said.

Chapter - 35

"No one is here, let's go inside."

"You all go first, I'll keep a watch," said Ravi.
"Okay, if anyone comes. Let us know."
"Will do!... Now go!"

They went inside the same way, a couple of minutes later Ravi joined them too. They knew where to go, so they straight climbed to the third floor, but to their surprise, the police had moved all the files to some other place. The room was all empty.

"Shit!" said Shreya.
"What do we do now?" asked Maya.
"We all get separate and search the whole school."
"No way, I am going alone!" said Riya.
"We can't find out together, we don't have enough time," said Shreya.

"It's not like we can chill here all night. We have to leave before anyone comes!" said Maya.

"So, Riya and I will search this floor. Ravi and Mayank you search the second floor!"
"So... I search alone!" asked Maya.

"No... you keep watch on all of us, take everyone on the conference call. We will keep posting to each other, so we will know, where everybody is!"
"All of you have brought their hands-free? as I told you!" said Shreya, wearing hers.
"Yeah!" replied all.

"So, I am going to the principal room. I will be sitting at the center of the school, outside the principal's office. So, I could keep watch on all of you, and if anything goes south, run straight towards the principal office" said Maya and took all of them on a conference call.

"Check!…check! 123...! 123...! Can you hear me?"
"Yeah, Ravi we all can hear you, loud and clear."
"Good and I too can hear all of you. Let's begin with a joke"
"Hainnn…! A joke... at this time!"
"Seriously… Ravi."
"What… I am just trying to lighten the mood, guys."
"Okay go on," said Maya.
"Once... chiti and Hathi decided to get married, but the chiti's parents said no to the boy. Guess why?" he asked.
"Why?" everyone asked in one voice.

"You guys didn't even try to guess."

"Just tell us and move on... Ravi!"

"Fine, they said 'No' because the boy's teeth were outside his mouth!" said and laughed so loud it echoed in the whole building.

"Shhhh…keep quiet!!" said Shreya.

"And don't tell any more jokes, please!" said Riya.

"You guys are so boring!!" said Ravi in sarcasm.

"Go on, move. We have a lot to do...!"

They went as planned the initial moments were fine but then Shreya and Riya saw something.

"What the fuck is that?" said Shreya pointing at the tree.

"What is it... what do you guys see?" asked Maya.

"It looks like a boy!... Of around seven or eight. Hanging from the tree upside down like a bat!", described Riya.

"What?"

"What the fuck…!"

"Be careful guys..." said Maya.

"Yeah, we will"

"I am going near the window to take a better look!" said Shreya and walked further.

"I am with her", Riya also said.

"Guys…!"

"What…Ravi, do you see anything too. Tell us?"

"No, I wanted to say... it feels like we all are in a movie, on a mission, right?"

"Ravi!!…see the situation!!"

"I will keep him shut...don't worry!"

"Yeah, you do that, Mayank. Please!"

"Okay… okay, I will stay quiet!"

"Yeah, you better!" said Riya.

"I am at the window, I can still see him. His eyes are closed, looks like he's sleeping" said Shreya, fear was present in her voice but not in her bravery.

"Yeah, it looks scary as hell!" said Riya.

"Don…don't do that Riya!" Shreya said in a panicked voice.

"What…What happened?"

"Riya moved torch at him, and I think he woke up….Run! Riya!" said Shreya.

"What is going on there guys? Are you alright!" said Mayank.

"Yeah! Can you hear me, Shreya…? Riya?" said Maya.

"Mayank, I think we should go check on them?"

"No, I will go!"

"No! You stay there, Maya. We got it...!"

"Okay, but be careful...!"

"Let's go!" said Ravi.

"What is it… guys? Can you see them, are they fine?"

"No, Maya we cannot see them. There is no one here... the room is empty!" replied Ravi.

"What…where did they go? They were just there a minute ago!"

"Yeah... but now there is no one here, Maya!" said Mayank, fear in his voice made Maya more worried.

"Let me see at the tree, they were talking about"

"Let's check it."

"There is no one on the tree. It's just tree…"

"What the hell happened here?" said Mayank.

"I think guys, he got them!!" said Ravi, now sweating.

Chapter - 36

"I am coming guys, wait for me!", said Maya running towards them.

"Don't! Stay there! Hello… Maya…stay there!", said Ravi getting anxious.
"What happened? Is she coming?"
"I don't know man, she isn't answering...!"
"Let's get out of this room..."
"Yeah..."
"Maya…! Maya…! Can you hear me?" asked Ravi shouting her name.
"Dude, she is nowhere to be found...!"
"Yeah Mayank, Shreyaaaa…! Riyaaa…! Can anyone hear me?"
"Stop it...Ravi, there is no one to answer. Where the hell the girls go?"
"And why only girls…. Why not us?"
"So what should we do now?"

"I don't know, Ravi..."
"Maybe we should go out and tell the police…!"
"Tell what, that we were trespassing and our friends got missing. They will lock us up!"
"So what do we do, now?"
"We have to find them, ourselves!"

"Okay, I will check this floor! You check the below one then... meet me at the principal's office. in half an hour, Okay?"
"Got it, best of luck man!"

"You too," said Ravi, and they got split. They all decided to stay together but in the first hour of their investigation, they were now all alone, each and everyone was on their own.

"There is nobody here!" said Mayank in the hands-free, they were still connected, but only Mayank and Ravi were audible.
"Here too, is nothing!" replied Ravi.
"Wait… I saw something!"
"What Mayank, what is It...? Talk to me!" "What is it?"
"Shhh… keep quiet, there is someone in this room, I think!"
"Where are you?"
"Classroom of VI-B, on the second floor."
"Got it… hang on, I am coming!"
"No, stay there… I got it!!"
"Don't try to be heroic, I am coming…!"

"Hmm…" was the only reply Ravi got, he instantly ran towards the room but got stuck because something or someone was walking in circles right in front of the stairs.

He thought of flashing a light on it but didn't, just slowly walked towards it, scared as shit. His big muscular body was trembling in fear; he never got this scared in his life. His feet were like jammed in cement, every step was harder to take than the last one. His breath was audible to his ears, so was his heartbeat, looking down at the ground from the third floor, he thought of jumping for a moment but didn't, that would have meant instant death, and there was still a chance and whatever that was will leave him alone or at least alive.

As he got closer, he felt something cold under his nose, it was blood coming from the nose. He panicked at seeing blood on his fingers, ran away from the thing but it grabbed his foot and he fell. Then all went black.

Mayank went near to see, what was there. There seemed to have a shadow of a woman, sitting and doing something on the floor, as he got closer he felt like she was drawing something with her finger. Silently sitting and drawing, she didn't even care he was there, he was now standing right behind her, using a flashlight he tried to see, what was she doing, but he fell back as soon as he saw. She was writing 'MAYANK' from blood, he ran in the opposite direction but she opened her mouth which smelled like a rotten corpse and made him vomit, he vomited blood which freaked him out, even more, she was like sucking him in her mouth like a vacuum.

She completely sucked him in her mouth while he broke a nail trying to hold a pillar. Now all of our gang was gone just like that, they went inside and now school was empty as it was before they came. Everything went back to normal, no ghosts, no blood, nothing at all, and it was like nothing happened there few hours back. All the doors got closed and windows too even their footprints and fingerprints were erased from the scene.

Chapter - 37

"Sir, I told you nobody came. We were here all night", said a constable to the inspector, who came to see school the next day.

"Shut up... and open the door!"

"Okay sir..." he said and opened the front door.

"Hmm…there was someone here last night," he said looking suspiciously at him.

"How could there had been anybody, we were here all night. We didn't even leave for a minute."

"Hmm…" …. "Something happened here last night, I can feel it."

"What… feel it! But how sir?" the constable said, trying to control his smile.

"Go outside and do your work," he said in response.

"What work, sir?"

"Anything, just leave me alone for a while. GO!"

"Okay sir," he said and left him alone.

"There was someone here, I can sense it but there is no proof, no clues of any kind, no evidence"…He was thinking. 'What is this? it's a piece of cloth, most probably a stall, someone wearing it was here last night. He put it in an evidence bag. There are no footprints, even when the school hasn't been cleaned since the investigation began, there is dust on every door, window, and floor but still no footprints', and 'How can someone walk without leaving prints behind?'

"There is a strange smell in the air, like a perfume or deodorant. Someone wearing it was here; it's still in the air, faint but still present. Constables said that nobody came, so how it's possible for this place to have a smell and a piece of cloth here?"

There was nothing on the first floor, but as he walked further on the second floor he saw dragging marks on the floor. "Someone was dragged from here to there!'… 'What is it on the pillar? Looks like someone's fingernail, most probably from a hand"… He saw a room whose door was closed but the handle was clean like it was recently opened. 'How the hell... is this handle clean?' 'Room is empty but it was recently opened, maybe last night'. 'What is it on the window? It looks like blood, and it's fresh, crusted but fresh!'… He took a sample of it too. There was another blood mark on the floor like someone fell there and then was dragged backward as the marks showed. He tried to take a sample of it too, but couldn't, blood was dried up, probably was older.

"There was someone or more than one person here last night!"

he said to the constable who was drinking his morning tea.
"*Chai* sir…!" he asked, holding a cup.

"No thanks! As I was saying... there were people here. You said nobody came, so how did I find these then?" he said showing him evidence bags.
"Wh…where did you find these?"
"Inside the school… Where else..!"
"There was no one, sir. I can assure you, tell him, Suresh…" he told to the other constable.
"Yes sir, he is telling the truth. Nobody came here, we were up all night."
"So, how did I find these, do you think I am lying!" he said, angrily.
"No…no sir, we didn't say that!"
"Maybe, somebody came in when we left for the bathroom. We were gone just for a minute!"
"Both of you... at the same time…why?"
"We…we…"
"Stop, I don't want to hear it. Tell forensics to sweep this whole place, I want everything checked for prints of any kind...!"

"Okay sir, we will," they said and saluted, he left.

"I told you not to leave, but you said it will be fine!"
"It was probably nothing. He is just a little crazy, as I have heard!" he said indicating it with his finger, moving in circles to side his forehead.

"If he found, that we were gone all night. We will be suspended!"

"Don't worry, he won't. Nobody takes him seriously; everyone thinks he is a little crazy..."

"If anything goes wrong, it will be on you!"

"Okay, fine!"

Chapter - 38

"Inspector Anand, what is the status of that school case?" asked Commissioner.

"Sir, I am handling it myself. We have made some good progress and found some clues..."

"What about that security guard?"

"We haven't found anything regarding him. We are doing our best and I assure you we will find something, soon enough!"

"Do something fast, I am getting pressure from superiors. School's principal had made some good contacts in these years and he is putting pressure on my superiors, who are putting it on me. So work fast!"

"Don't worry sir, I will!" he saluted and left the cabin.

"Hello, commissioner speaking!" "As you said, I have put pressure on him to close the case soon, no…! Don't worry it will be closed soon enough. Just remember what you promised…Huh. Don't worry... I remember mine!" he said and put his phone down.

"I am sure; something is pretty big, behind this. That we haven't found yet!" said Anand to his fellow officer.

"Yes sir, you are probably right because some things just don't match or connect...!"

"Yeah, Tavde... but we have to find something soon, or this case will go cold. I am getting pressure from the commissioner!"

"Don't worry sir, we will. The forensic report will be here anytime, now"… "Maybe, it will shine some light on the case..."

"Let's see, why isn't it here yet?"
"I just called the lab; they told me the report is on the way...!"
"Good…"… "Get it to me as soon it reaches!"
"Okay, sir!"

"Hmmm… the report says the blood I found was from one person and the nail was from another, there were two different blood from two different people, then that nail and that piece of cloth had different D.N.A. from all of them...!" he said reading a file in his hand.

"So sir, according to this... there were four people, there last night!"

"No Tavde, there were five!"

"But sir, how?"

"I also contacted Telephone Company to track the cell activity from last night. It shows there were five phones activated last night at school..."

"So, where did they go?... why didn't constables see them coming or leaving?"

"Ohh… those constables are useless, they are probably lying that they were on duty the whole time."

"It could be possible!"… "Should I initiate the search for them?"

"No benefit! They went in but they didn't leave. Not even one of them."

"What!!... Where did they go then?"

"I have no idea but we have to find out. They could be in some kind of danger!"

"How would we find them…? I think we should call a 'Baba' or something!"

"What… why?"

"I think that place is haunted... so probably a '*Baba* or some *Tantrik* will be able to help...".

"No Tavde, he will just fool us and waste our time. We don't need a Baba..."

"So, where do we begin?"

"Where it all happened…at school!"

"But that place has been fully swept. There would be nothing...!"

"We don't need a clue. We need something more than that..."

"Like what, sir?"

"I am going to spend a night at school, probably tonight. Let's see if something comes up!"
"What… night at that place, where five people just vanished into thin air. I don't think so; it would be a good idea sir!"…
"Take me with you!"
"No, I can't put your life in danger. I will go alone..."
"What danger sir, it's my duty… please let me come."
"Fine, you can come!"

Chapter - 39

"Sir, you want something. I have wafers and biscuits and some chips!" Tavde said holding a bag in his hand.

"What…. Tavde, I told you... we are going on an investigation not on a picnic...!"

"But sir, if we are going to stay here all night. It'd better not to be empty stomach"… "And we die; I don't want to die hungry."

"Nobody is going to die, just set the perimeter, first."

"Already done sir!"

"Good… then give some chips, I am hungry too," he said, Tavde gave him a packet and they both laughed.

"So sir, what could we expect to see, tonight?"

"I don't know, Tavde…. I don't know!"

"Sir, if anything goes south. I have told my wife to not worry about me."

"Don't worry Tavde…. nothing will happen!"

"What you say... Should we look around?"

"No, it would be safe if we just stay here."
"Got it..." said Tavde, they were sitting in the middle of school like camping.
"Did you hear something....?"
"No, nothing sir...what is it?"
"I don't know... it sounds like someone's crying."
"Why can't I hear it?"
"You can't... anything?"
"No sir..."

"Give me the torch, I will go and see if there's something" he walked towards one of the classrooms, it was closed but he could hear someone inside, the cry was as clear for him to hear as his racing pulse. He has been in the police for a small period, though he was not of the scared kind but, because of his strange supernatural ability, sometimes it gets hard for him to retain his fear.

Since he was a kid, he could see and hear things, others can't. It used to strike fear in him, enough that he used to close him up in his room for days but now he was grown up and much more experienced with that kind of stuff. When he was maybe five or six years old, he was once playing hide and seek with his friends, he hid inside a place that was once had been a post office, now was just ruins. He knew not to hide at that place, as his mother had told him not to, but he couldn't think of any place because he fell when he ran to hide while the counting was on because of the shortage of time he went there.

He saw a man stamping something alone in the whole

building his head was down and it looked like he was deeply indulged in his work. Anand went near him to tell him, that he is just playing and had not come to steal anything. As he went near him, he smelled something awful, he was so young that he didn't know what it was but it was something he had never smelled before. His feet went cold even it was early August, the man was stamping on letters, he called him but the man didn't respond so he shook his shoulder and suddenly that sound of *Thak...thak....thak...* of stamping went silent. His head was still down but when he turned his face towards Anand, the scream was the only sound thing that came out of Anand, as he fainted.

When his friends and others came to him after hearing the scream, he was unconsciously lying on the ground, they woke him up and he told them that he saw a man there whose lower jaw was hanging down from his face and he didn't have a nose.

Though they told him it was just his illusion, he knew what he saw, it was as clear to him as the sun in the daytime. He may or may not have forgotten that incident, but he definitely never played hide and seek again.

After some years another incident like this happened, he was then maybe nine years old. He was out to buy a project file for his schoolwork; it was night-time, past 9 pm. Not many people were on the street because of the cold of December, he was alone on that street, where the shop was. The view was clear but foggy under the yellow street light, rubbing his hands he was walking towards the shop when he saw someone was walking towards him, and it didn't particularly raise an alarm in him because he thought it was someone else, going somewhere. The street was all empty except for few dogs that were sleeping there on the side, as the man came close and close, the dogs woke up.

Started growling and then eventually barking at the man coming, he didn't respond to it, he was walking fearlessly as calmly as a river before the storm. Anand got scared not of the man but from the dogs, even though they weren't barking at him. Then dogs started barking loudly, stood up and took an attacking position, still, they didn't run towards the man, they were jumping and barking at their same spots, the man was walking for quite a while now, the street was not that long but he was taking like forever to reach near him, though he didn't stop not even for a sec.

One of the dogs started barking at Anand, he immediately stopped walking; he was standing in the middle of the street, a street light pole was behind him. The light was shining right above him casting his big shadow in front of the dogs, dogs didn't have one. The louder the dog barked at him the more he got stunned, he looked at the dog, right in his shining green eyes, looking like an emerald. He somehow understood that the dog didn't mean any harm to him, but was like trying to help. Only for a moment, their eyes met and again the dog started staring at the man.

The man just came near him and stopped, his hands crossed

and head down. He didn't utter a word, dogs were out of control like they will tear him apart but didn't, they wanted to, but like something was stopping them. He was too scared to move, sounds of barking were all he could hear and then the man raised his head, there were red eyes and no teeth, just a very long tongue, swinging outside his mouth. There were marks on his face like he just got out of a car crash, blood was still present in those wounds, but there was no pain on his face. The man spoke to him "Can you give me blood…? I want blood! Your blood….! Give me your blood!" "I can smell blood running in your veins, it makes me hungry!" he said and licked his lips.

Anand screamed so loud, that for a second, even dogs stopped barking. As he woke up from falling unconscious he was alone in the street.

Chapter - 40

He opened the door, there was no one inside but the sound of crying was getting closer and closer. He went inside and a gust of wind closed the door behind him, though he was scared, but, now he was used to, this kind of stuff. The flashlight also started blinking and then died, total darkness and nothing else could be seen, he tried to open the door but couldn't. Sitting on a bench, as he searched from his hands, he was thinking that maybe someone was trying to talk to him, he started hearing multiple voices, boy and girl then a grown man's voice was there and then shouting and screaming of children, putting his hands on ears, Anand tried to shut the sound but couldn't. The voices were getting louder and louder and unbearable to hear, now blood was dripping from his ears. He screamed, but the voices didn't stop until he kicked the door and got out, breathing heavily, his ears were hurting and so was his head. Blood was still dripping but was now slow and then stopped, he immediately got up and ran towards, Tavde.

"What happened, Sir...? "Are you all right?"
"Yeah, I am fine…" he said, catching his breath.
"Here...drink it, Sir…!"
"Thank you…!"
"What happened… what did you see?"
"I went… into a classroom… and, there was screaming… multiple voices of different people, and it got unbearable. My ears started bleeding, somehow I got out..."
"Was anyone there, too…?"
"No, Tavde. Just voices!"
"Breath!… Sir, Breath!". "Should we leave now…?"
"No, Tavde… we have to stay!"
"But sir…"
"No, we have to...!"
"Okay, Sir….as you say."
"Let's eat first…, what you got there in the bag?"
"I got plenty, Sir…"
"You really, came prepared…huh!" he said and they both laughed.

There was no interference for the rest of the night. They stayed, searched the whole school but nothing strange happened again. Now that was strange, stranger than they had expected. The next morning they were out, the night was turned out to be a total waste. But as he was going to exit the main school entrance he heard "Anand…. Anand…." Someone was calling out his name. He turned but there was nobody; Tavde was already outside, standing near the car, probably talking to his wife.

"Is someone there…?" he asked looking around, but it was deserted not even a creature was there. He heard again "Anand….Anand…come here…". "Hello, is anyone there…? It's inspector Anand… do you need help…?" he walked further. "I will help you… please don't be afraid. Come out!" Nobody came out, so he walked further and ended up going backside of the school, the sun was up, and it was morning, so no reason to be afraid.

"Who… is there? I am the police, please come out!" he said when something ran from behind him swiftly. Again nobody answered, so he went near the canteen, the sound was coming from inside, like something being scratched. The door was open, but there was no one inside but the sound of scratching was still coming, then he looked up.

There was something hanging from the ceiling like a bat, but it wasn't a bat. It was a human or at least looked like one, black as night, only his eyes were shining green like an emerald. It looked like he was scraping on something, there was something in his mouth but it was hard to see. It was a bone, Anand got shocked and moved a little back, as his foot hit a can, the thing, up at the ceiling heard it, the bone fell from his mouth and came rolling at Anand's feet.

Now that thing was gazing at him, he didn't move but his eyes were stuck on the door, he would have shouted but, what if that thing gets angry and attacked him.

Tavde started looking for him and shouted his name but didn't get an answer. Anand was now getting anxious about, if that thing heard Tavde, it could attack him.

"What are you doing here, Sir...? I was waiting outside!" Tavde said and that thing jumped on Anand, he screamed. Tavde ran inside...

Chapter - 41

"What do we do now…? Sir!"
"I don't know, Tavde… I don't know..." Anand said, his hand was on his head which was bleeding.
"Where are we, anyway….?"
"I think we are in the same place but at a different time!"
"What… how do you know?" he asked getting anxious.
"Look there… that building wasn't there when we came last night. It is now..."
"Yeah… it wasn't there" "How the hell, did that happen…! How did we get here?" "Maybe... we are at some other place!"
"No… Tavde, we are at the same place, look... the school building is the same, just before it was renovated but, it's still the same building..."
"How did we get here…?"
"That, I don't know…!"
"It means we travelled in time…somehow?" Tavde said, scratching his head.
"Looks like it…!"

"Should we call someone?"
"That won't work, Tavde. All the people we know from the police department, either has not joined police yet or wouldn't know us, because according to them, we are not police…"
"But why…?"
"Think carefully, Tavde...! You and I weren't in the police department when the school hadn't been renovated. It looks like… we are at least ten years back in time!"
"What!!!... Ten years", Tavde shouted.
"Yes, Ten years….! Tavde. Let's go outside!"
"What would we do now…? I am scared, Sir!"
"First we get ourselves checked… then, we will think of something"… "My head hurts; it probably needs stitches and your hand too..."
"My hand…?"
"Yeah, look there. You are bleeding…!"
"Oh shit!!... I didn't notice. Now it's hurting!" he said looking at his scratched hand.
"Let's... go to the doctor first!"
"Okay, sir…"

They walked from the back to the front of the school, everything was changed. The school didn't look the same as they remembered it from last night, the paint was different, not new but not the same color and the doors were also of different color, and in the guard's room there was someone not Sandeep. They knew his face; he was a man of old age maybe in his forties in a security guard dress, perfectly cleaned and well ironed. The school was empty but why it should be crowded with students, the sun was shining at the top of their heads. The heat was unbearable more for them as they were wearing warm clothes because of the cold temperature, back at where they came from. Now it was summer may be at its peak time, they immediately took off their sweaters and other warm things, and folded their sleeves to the elbow.

As the guard saw them coming, he ran towards them and asked who they were and what were they doing there. They told him that, they were cleaning back there and they fell on the water, spilled on the floor, they were in casuals because of the night out at school, so he believed them.

"Sir, I am hungry. Can we eat something first?"
"Tavde… everything around us changed, we have no idea what to do or where to go but your craving for food is still the same..."
"Don't laugh sir. What do I do... if I get hungrier when stressed!"
"Okay fine, let's eat something. I also have to take medicine, doctor told me to eat something before taking these, so let's eat."
"But, how would we be able to buy something?"
"Tavde, we are ten years back in time, not ten decades... money is still the same!"
"No sir, it is not, because you remember, govt. banned old 500 and 1000 rupees notes and people from now wouldn't take new ones. They would consider them as fake!"
"Shit! You are right? I didn't think of it. So what do we do now?" he was anxious now.
"I have some notes of 10, 20 & 50 Rs. I think they would work fine but we will only be able to buy street food…." He said

looking at Anand.

"Your mind works much better when it comes to food, fine! I will eat street food, it's not like we have other options!"

"Let's eat samosa…!"

"Whatever you want… we will eat whatever you want!" he said smiling.

"Sahab… you don't look from here. Are you new?" asked Paan wala to Tavde.

"Yeah, we just came today from Mumbai!" answered Anand.

"Do you need any help in finding a place to stay?" he further inquired, as he spread "Kattha" with his finger on Paan leaf.

"Yeah… yes, we would be grateful for any help...!"

"There is a room vacant for rent at my place. If you want you could stay there..." Paan wala replied, while handing them over two Paan.

"It would be great… Thank you!"

"But, sir…!"

"What… Tavde, what is it…?"

"Sir, don't forget we don't have money, not enough for even a night...!" he whispered in his ear.

Chapter - 42

"Sir, I am worried about my wife. She would freak out, as I will not return home tonight...!"
"But... you told me, you had said to her not to worry, right?"
"Yes, sir but still, she is my wife, a typical Indian housewife, you don't know how they get over sensitive in case of their husbands!"
"Don't worry; she will be fine… after all, you are a police officer. You could get busy with some work, and forget to inform her..."
"I hope so, Sir… it happens this way," Tavde said, looking worried. They were lying on the floor of a small room, just big enough for two of them to sleep.
"Sir… how would we be able to go back?"
"I don't know, Tavde…"
"But you seem so relaxed…Why? How?"
"Why would I be worried?" "There is no benefit in being worried!"
"But there should be some strain on your face…. But there

is nothing…how?" "It seems like… it has happened to you before, hasn't it?"
"You can say that…" he said and turned sideways.

They showed their police ID to the Pan Shop owner and told him that, they have come here in search of a criminal and if they found him, his prize money (which was supposed to be 10,000 Rs.) will be given to him. He wasn't literate enough to understand that the ID was from the future, just saw the Emblem and agreed.

"What! How…?"
"It happened… when I was in college!"
"I was coming home from college one day. It was raining outside and I had forgotten my umbrella. I stopped under a bus stand to take shelter, a girl came, she also didn't have an umbrella. She came and stood near me and suddenly the wind started blowing furiously, it was so fast that it became hard to stand under...

In a gust of wind, it felt like something changed but couldn't point out what. As the wind got slow a bit, I saw that the surroundings were changed, the bus stand became brand new and there were no shops near it. That girl then walked after the rain stopped, and I felt a strange urge to follow her, I didn't want to but something made me. I followed her to an old abandoned house, where she showed me how she died, and after that I was back to my time, unharmed…"
"What!!!... She showed you how she died?"
"Yeah… that!"

"How…?"
"Just like a movie, but only this time… I was in the movie, feeling and living everything!" he said.
"Whoah!!!!" he said by making an 'O' with his lips. "So, that's why you are not scared or shocked, you are used to it…"
"Yeah… you can say that".
"So, you think we would be able to go back this time, too…?"
"Let's see…"

The next morning they went back to school inquired if any children had gone missing or not. They found out nobody was missing till that moment, which meant that they arrived earlier than the abductions. The abductions started happening on that very day, but they couldn't catch the kidnapper because it would change the course of history and that would not be okay. So instead, they just followed them as they abducted one of the children, from their way going back home, they took the child into an old abandoned factory, and then they vanished, disappeared just like that into thin air.

Chapter - 43

Our gang, who got vanished from school, after a deadly encounter with the supernatural, was now in the middle of nowhere, in some woods. There was nothing around them but trees and trees of all sizes, small, medium, and large ones.

"Where the hell are we…?"
"How do you think I know, Mayank?"
"I am not asking you, Shreya. I am just murmuring..."
"So, keep your murmur inside your mouth. I don't want to hear a single word from your mouth...!"
"Okay… Okay… don't start a fight now, you guys. Just shut up my head hurts…"
"Mine too…" said Ravi, rubbing his forehead.
"All of us have a mild headache, I don't know why but it seems like it…"
"Yeah, Maya is right. My head hurts too but you know what hurts the most, my hand…!"
"Here… take it and cover it up, before it gets infected!" said

Maya and gave her muffler to Mayank, which he tied around his bloody hand.

"I swear… If I lose my hand, I am gonna kill all of you!"

"Why us…?"

"Why? Because it happened... coz of you, I told you we should not go into school again but you didn't listen!"

"You said… what?" "As much as I remember you were the one who wanted to go to school…"

"Just, shut up guys…" Ravi screamed, his head was hurting but not more than his chin.

"How long do you guys think we have been here?"

"I have no idea… maybe a couple of hours or maybe days, who knows…!"

"But how we got here in the middle of the jungle, we all were in school last night…"

"I just remember falling and hitting my chin… after that, it all went black…"

"But, here is day…we were at school, last night… It means we passed more than a couple of hours but maybe not days…!" said Mayank, holding his hand.

"Yeah… but, are we still in our world or some other world…!"

"It clearly, seems to have oxygen… so it means we are still on Earth," said Shreya.

"Thank God…" said Ravi.

"Do anyone have a watch… my phone seems to have died. Tell me time…"

"My phone is also dead…"

"Mine too…"

"I have a watch... but it's not working, it just stopped at 12:45… the time we went into school last night, it seems it stopped working the moment we entered the school but I didn't notice itthen…"

"Maya, what happened with you…?" asked Shreya.

"Yeah… you were on the lookout!"

"I don't clearly remember what happened… I am sorry,"

"Doesn't matter… we have more serious issues at hand. It looks like, it's going to be dark soon, we need to find a shelter… we can't stay here!"

"Yeah... let's walk. See… If we could find a place to stay…!"

"A place...! Are you serious Maya, we are in the middle of woods" ."We have to look… we can't stay here…"

"Fine… let's go!"

"Please, stop!! Guys… I can't walk further!"

"Don't be dramatic queen, Ravi… we have to walk".

"Yeah, Ravi… get up".

"You all go… I will stay here".

"No… I can't".

"We can't leave you behind…" said Maya, standing by a tree. "It's getting dark…". "Fine… let's walk!" said Ravi, getting up.

Chapter - 44

They walked maybe around 5 kilometers, then they found an abandoned old hut. It wasn't the best choice to stay but beggars can't be choosers, so they stayed there for the night. "Guys… I am hungry. Do we have something to eat?" said Riya.

"No…nothing. We have a couple of branches to burn, these strange trees don't have any fruit on them, just branches that too without fruit or leaves!" said Shreya, looking at a stack of branches.

"What do we do now?" said Maya; there was terror in her voice, which was getting lower because of hunger.

"I went out to look for a road or something to eatbut there is no sign of any road or life…. Nothing to eatnot even animals!" "Eww!! Are you out of your mind Mayank, we can't eat animals…"

"Yeah… she is right. I am not going to eat anything, alive!"
"I am just saying, guys. It's not like I am cooking a rabbit, for God's sake!"

"But he got a point… we need to eat, something, anything!!!" said Ravi, looking scratching their names on the wall with a rock.

"And… what the hell are you doing…?"
"I am carving our names if we die. People would need to know we were here…"
"Who the hell do you think is coming to find us?"
"I don't know… anybody. Forest department, police… anyone"

"But nobody knows where we were. We all left for the reunion and never returned…" "We didn't tell anyone, where we were staying… no one knows and no one ever gonna find us here…" said Shreya, worried and shocked after hearing her own words.

"Yeah… only God knows where we are!" said Maya.
"Shut up… someone will come and find us… I am not ready to die not here…" said Riya, murmuring.

"We are not going to die… just shut up!!" shouted Mayank.
"Guys please, we have to hold it together… we can't lose our minds. We need them, to get out of here!" said Maya; it was like a scene from a horror movie, in which every character starts losing their sanity, because of the difficult circumstances.

Everyone was losing their sanity, acting strange, maybe projecting their inner fears towards the situation.

Days passed, maybe two or three, I don't know exactly, and they were starving to death. They even tried to eat branches and even wood from the hut but couldn't, just put it in their mouth and vomited. The situation got more serious because their water got over, now it was starvation with dehydration. "Guys!!!... Wake up, see I found water…!"

"Where... where… Mayank…?" asked Riya, looking around bewildered.

"There… look…!" he said, pointing towards something.

Chapter - 45

It was their second day, back in past, the trip turned out to be useless because they couldn't get any clues or any witnesses, and they would not be considered a witness in court, because they exactly didn't see any face or found any place, where the children were being held captive. They had to go home now because there was no point in staying any longer, people would have noticed their absence by now.

The question was how, how to go back to the future? So they decided to go back to school, in hope that they would find a way to go back but on their way back to school, they witnessed another kidnapping but a little differently, they saw a face this time. Following him turned out to be useless, as he went into the same abandoned factory and disappeared again.

Again next night they sneaked into school, now it was time to go back, they can't stay here for long. The school was empty and dark, as they had expected, but to their amazement, there were people inside the school. In black and red robes with strange markings painted over their faces, with what looked like, blood. They were chanting something and then they brought a man, beaten up badly and tied down, then they placed him between the star made on the ground and he was trying to run but couldn't, they made something on his head with red color or don't know what. With a slash of a knife, they beheaded him and his head rolled down, eyes gouged out, rolling on the ground.

Tavde almost ran to stop them but was stopped by Anand, as much as he wanted to stop them too, they couldn't. They couldn't mess with time. After that, they cleaned the place, without leaving a drop behind, they should try for house cleaning business, they very much had chances of success. Then, one of the men was also seen carrying a woman (who looked unconscious) out with him.

After that, they went again to the canteen but there wasn't that creature this time. They couldn't find a way to go back but then they went into the school building; something was sitting on the stairs, which were leading down to the first floor. "What the hell is that…?" asked Tavde. "How would I know?" replied Anand and indicated him to keep quiet. They got closer to it, they heard the sound of scratching, that thing didn't have a head and suddenly it turned towards them immediately with shock they ran backward while keep falling.

They saw that man, who was just beheaded with his head in his hands. He was scratching and peeling its skin, off it, trying to fix his eyes back in place but wasn't able to do that. The scene was so hideous; they couldn't see it again and instantly got out of the school building, panting vigorously. They saw it again but this time, sitting on the front porch of the school door, again they ran backward. They could hear their heart beating louder than a jet plane's noise, felt like it will burst out of their chest. Finally, they fainted, fell, and lost consciousness, sweating heavily, the last scene Anand saw before closing his eyes, was that thing coming towards them with its head in its hands.

Chapter - 46

"I am starving… I am parched. I need something to eat and drink…!"
"So… what do you think I am doing here?"... "I am trying to get water for us. Just keep quiet and help…!"
"Okaaaay…. Just do it fast!"
"What do you want me to do, Ravi… jump in it?" said Shreya, getting frustrated because she was trying to pull up the bucket from into the well, but it was taking for ever to come out.
"Let me do it… I am strong…"
"Fine… do it," Shreya handed over the rope to Mayank.
"Why the hell… is it taking so long…?"
"But you were strong… I thought you would do it, in one try!"
"Don't give me sarcasm, Riya. You think you are better… here you do it!"
"Are we playing passing the parcel… just let one person do it. Please…" Maya said, her head was spinning because of the lack of water in her body.

"Look… I can see it. I can see the bucket guys…" screamed Mayank.

"Pull up faster…!"
"I am trying…"
"Let us all help you… come on guys" .
"On three…1…2…3… Pull…pull…!"
"What the hell is it… it's not water…?" Ravi said, spitting.
"Yeah... it's not water!"
"What the hell is this thing…?"
… Said Shreya, looking inside the bucket.
"What is it…?"
"It's mud… not water but slimy mud".
"After 20 min of pulling … we pulled out this!" said Riya and kicked the bucket.
"It's because of you Mayank…" said Shreya.
"Why me… what did I do?"
"You said, it was water… because of you we did this useless task of pulling… and now my hand also hurts"
"I just said what I saw… I thought it was water. How would I know, it wasn't water?"
"Shut…. Up…"
"Just shut upguys…"
"Yeah… spoke the so-called mother… go on tell us what we should do now, Mother…"
Go to hell! said Maya.

A couple of hours later, they were not even in a condition to move or speak. Lips were dry like desert, losing skin that they were removing intentionally, God knows why. They didn't

even try to get back to the hut, just laid down right there near the well like dead bodies.
"Are… are you guys still alive…?"
"Who is this… asking?"
"Don't know… who I am. Well, who are you…?"
"I am snake…"
"Ohh… yeah I know you. Nice to meet you… I am frog!"
"Guys… I am fish, nice to meet you…!"
"I am monkey… huhhh!"
"Stay away from me… I am eagle… shuuuuu…!"
Stay away from me. You deadly bird…"
"Yeah… frog is right… … flesh-eating flying devil…"
"Shut up you animal without legs…"
"I don't need leg...s…s…"

"I think the snake finally died…" said the Monkey and laughed strangely.
"Good… she was idiot…huhhhh".
"I am going on the tree… you guys coming?"
"Are you serious!!..." said Frog.
"Hahahaha… I forgot you have tiny legs… you can't climb… huhhh!"
"Shut up…!"
"I am coming…. You climb. I fly… shuuuuu"
"Good… see you up there…"
''I am going into well…" said the Frog in anger.

"Hey, fish… what happened to you. Are you coming with me…?"… "Hello… fish. Are you there…? Looks like the fish is already dead…good…"

You all would be wondering where these animals came from, so there was no animal. It was our gang, who, because of dehydration and hunger had gone crazy. The snake was Shreya, the frog was Ravi, Monkey was Mayank and the eagle was Riya, and Maya was fish.

Chapter - 47

'There was never been a person in those woods in the last 100 years, except the people who already live here called "Mahatos". People who believed to be worshippers of "Asmodeus", an evil entity who opposes the work of God.

This was the first paragraph written in Omayun. Which our gang found in the room (laying on a podium of what seemed to be pure gold), in which they were being held. After they turned into animals and went crazy, they were captured by the people who lived there. Strange looking people, pale in color, without clothes, bare and nude. They had no hair; even their women were nude and bald, making them creepier.

"Where the hell… are we?" said Ravi, panting.
"I think somebody got to us!"
"But why the hell… are we tied?" asked Riya.
"I think they are locals…"
"I thought no one lives here…"

"That's what we all thought... Mayank!"
"I can't untie my rope... can you?"
"No... it's so tight"
"Do you guys feel a little strange...? I was starving but not anymore!" said Maya, shocked.
"Yeah... I don't feel hungry too....How...why?"
"Me too..." said Mayank.
"I also..."
"But I do... I still feel hungry..." said Riya.

"What... why only you are hungry but all of us feel full?" They all were tied up in a room made out of wood with no electricity, not even a bulb. There were torches lit and hung in the center of every wall, the room was empty but there was a podium on which there was a book, at first they couldn't read it but then it started to translate itself into English. Words started to change their shapes and designs and because their hands were tied on the back they couldn't turn the page then two strange-looking people came into the room, looked at them, touched them and then took the book with them, on their way, the light from torch shined on the book and Shreya read its name, it was 'Omayun', she remembered it instantly, it was the book Mansukh Uncle's wife told them about.

"Are they even human...?"
"I don't think so".
"No... they were human but not from our time. I have read about people who used to live in ancient India they were described in the book almost same as the people we saw..." said Riya.

"Where the hell did you read that…?"
"I read it in the library of our school… shit! (She murmured)"
"What!!! School… you said you work in an MNC?" asked Ravi.
"That's not the question now…"
"No… tell us".
"Okay… sorry I lied…!"
"But why…?"
"Leave it… we have more dangerous issues at hand…" Shreya said, trying to stop them.
"Ohh… so you knew about it too…" said Mayank.
"Yeah… I do. So what…?"
"So you two are together in this lie….huh!"
"Yeah… Ravi we are together… okay. Just let it go and focus on where we are and who are these people…"
"She is right… guys just leave it" .
"Ohh… so you are in this too…huh, Maya!"
"No… I didn't know too, but it still doesn't matter… right now!"
"Why doesn't it matter… it does!"
"Guyyyyysssss…. Shut uppp…!" screamed Shreya. "Just leave it…" she said.
"Just hear what she has to say…"
"Fine…"
"I was saying that these people look ancient…"
"So… what do you want to say, Riya?"
"I think we are not in 2021 anymore…!" she said looking at their faces.

Chapter - 48

"What do you think, we should do now…?"
"I don't know Mayank… but we have to take that book and destroy it. Otherwise, others would find it and people would get hurt!"
"But how…?" asked Ravi. They all were hiding behind another hut, a little further from where they were being held. Those strange people were gathered together in a group. They were praying, a person was sitting on a throne and they were bowing down to him, he was wearing a crown.
"I think he is their leader…!" whispered Maya.
"I think so, too…"
"Look… there is the book…!." Said Riya, pointing towards (what looked like a temple).
"What is that place…?"
"I think it's a temple".
"But why of black color… temples usually are of white color or colorful but never black.
"Leave it… let's just take that book and get out of here!"

"Let's go quietly…"
"Move…" Shreya said and indicated them to move.

They moved quietly hiding behind from one hut to another. Those people were busy doing (whatever they were doing), they went into the temple and started looking around at the strange structure. There was a strange idol in the middle of the place; the temple wasn't painted black it was made up of some strange rock, nothing they had ever seen before. The idol was of some other strange material, it didn't look like a rock, either, it was metal but it was shining and looked made up of pure gold, but that wasn't gold. The idol wasn't of any God they knew but had a strange face looking like a dragon, red eyes like blood with no iris, two long teeth coming out of its mouth, long and sharp-pointed, and a hell of a lot of small teeth. Two arms with claws at their ends and instead of a human foot, it had hoofs, like a horse.

But there was one thing they all recognized instantly, that was the pendant on its neck. It was the same pendant.

"You all remember it…!" asked Ravi, strangely looking at the pendant.
"Yeah… I do. It looks the same as the one we saw at Mansukh Uncle's home" replied Shreya.
"Not same… it is that one!" argued Mayank.
"But how…?"
"Seriously… Riya, everything that had happened to us till now, if I see devil, live in front of me I wouldn't be surprised!"
"Yuppp… that's true"
"Don't touch it… Ravi…!"

"Hush…! Maya, or they will hear us..."
"Okay… just don't touch it!"
"I will be fine, don't worry…"
"You don't know that for sure…we don't know what that thing could be, and what it can do!"
"Ahhhh…!"
"What happened, Ravi… are you okay?"
"Sit… sit here. Tell us what happened!"
"I… I… saw something very strange and horrible…" said Ravi, he was panting and sweating.
"What was it…?" asked Riya.

He told them what he saw; he saw what Mansukh uncle's wife saw that day when she confronted him, that horrible vision from hell. Then they took the book and left, as they crossed the border of the temple they got caught and this time they didn't wake up in a hut but in a different place. This time they were in a place where those people, give human sacrifice in the name of the Devil, who they knew by a different name.
"What is this place…" asked Shreya, tied up with chains.
"I don't know… but it looks like blood on that wall"
"Yeah… but whose blood…?"
"Maybe of some animal…"
"I don't think so it's animal blood… I think it's human…!" said Ravi, terrified.

Chapter - 49

"Who is that person…? Isn't he the one they were bowing down to…?"
"Yeah… he is that!" Riya, looking terrified.
"But why is he all tied up, and looks pretty beaten too…"
"I don't understand it… and somehow don't you think he looks familiar!" Shreya said looking at him, trying to figure out where she has seen him before.
"No… I don't think so"
"Yeah… he doesn't look familiar to me…"
"Definitely, not...! Under all that makeup," Mayank said.
"Makeup… it's not makeup!" said Ravi, laughingly.
"Hello… hey…, are you okay?"Ravi asked and touched his foot with his own.
"I think, he is unconscious…"
"Yeah… he should be. If I were beaten that badly, I would be unconscious too!"
"Helloo… wake up, man… wake up!"
"Huhh… where I am…?" "Who are you…?" the man said,

looking here and there. His eyes were still not open fully.

"I am Ravi… who are you, and what are you doing here?"

"I… I… don't remember anything, my head hurts, and why I am all tied up?"

"You are being captive by strange-looking people…! Like we are!"

"Where I am…?"

"I don't know that…"

"Who are you, people…?"

"It's a long story… but for now, we are captives just like you,"

"Hmmm…"

"What are you doing here… how did you get here?" asked Maya.

"I don't recall exactly… I was at work, and then I woke up here..."

"Where do you work…?" asked Riya.

"At a school…"

"Where…?"

"At Laxmi Nagar…!"

"What is your name…?" asked Shreya, she finally recognized who he was.

"It's Sandeep…!!"

"What!!!...." everybody said in unison, shocked.

"See… I told you, he looked familiar. It's him, Sandeep…! Mansukh Uncle's son… guys!"

"What…! But how? You got disappeared from school… how did you get here?"

"You people know me…?"

"Yeah… that too, pretty good…"

"You have no idea... in how much trouble we went through... to find you," said Maya.

"But who are you... police?"

"No... We used to study at the school where you work. Back when Mansukh Uncle used to work there..." said Shreya.

"Yeah, after you went missing and some strange things happened at the school, our reunion got canceled and then we decided to find you, though we didn't find you, but, we found a lot of new things, about your family... their work and Mansukh Uncle..." said Riya.

"What did you find out exactly...?"

"Don't be so innocent... we found out the truth behind your father's innocent smile and dumb looks..."

"What...?"

"Guys... shhhh... shut up!" said Maya.

"Why...?" whispered Riya.

"Don't you remember that his mother told us, he doesn't know about all of this, he still thinks his father was a good man..."

"So what...?" "He should know the truth..." argued Riya and Shreya.

"Where are you taking him... stop!!!" screamed Ravi. The strange people were taking Sandeep, somewhere. They decided not to tell him the truth about his father because of two reasons; First: he would not trust them and Second: it's not their place to tell him the truth, it should be his mother who tells him, and they thought everybody deserves to have a good father. Let him live in his delusion.

"Leave him!!!... Leave him alone...!" screamed Maya.

"Where are you taking him...?" asked Riya.

"Where they took him?"

"I think they are going to sacrifice him...!" said Shreya, shocked and her face became pale.

Chapter - 50

"What should we do now...?"
"I don't know. My mind is not working..."
"But we have to save him... right?"
"Yeah... but how?"
"I say, let him pay for the sins of his father...!"
"Are you out of your mind...Shreya?"
"No... I am sane and sound, and what's wrong with it...?"
"Everything...!" said Maya.
"Yeah, she is right... we can't let him die. We have to save him!" said Mayank, looking worried and terrified.
"No...Shreya is right. Let him die... who knows how many innocent kids had his father murdered...!"
"But that doesn't mean...he needs to die for it. He is innocent...!"
"Guys...!"
"What now, Ravi?"
"When you all were fighting, I found a way to see what is happening outside. Come here...!"

"See... through this hole!" he said pointing towards the hole in the wall between two wooden planks with his eyes.

"Shreya was right, they are really... sacrificing him!" said Maya looking through the hole.

"We have to save him...!" "And I am not hearing any other arguments about this...!"

"Fine..." said both Riya and Shreya together.

"But how...?"

"That, we have to figure out Mayank, and soon..."

"Look for a way out...!"

"I see it... a door!"

"This is no time for jokes... Ravi, we all can see that door..."

"So, let's out by that..."

"How... genius...?"

"Look for something to cut these ropes... I have a plan!"

"Idiot!!!... These are not ropes. These are chains..."

"Yeah... they couldn't be cut easily," said Mayank.

"Think guys...! This is a sacrificial place. There must be big knives or axes or swords to cut a human head..."

"Yeah... that could cut through chain!"

"Start looking..."

"There is a cupboard... I could see it in the next room!"

"How will we go from this room to the next...?" Shreya said staring at Mayank.

"There is only one way..."

"What is it...?"

"One of us has to dislocate their thumb, that way he or she could be free and then go to the next room, find something and free us all..."

"Are you crazy...Ravi?"

"Are you out of your mind...? I am not going to do that...!"
"Do you have any better plans...?" he asked Shreya.
"No... I don't!" she replied looking down, frustrated and angry.
"Then... it is the plan... we have to act fast or by the time we reach there, they would have skinned him, by then..."
"Fine... who is going to do that?"
"I will...!" said Maya from behind.

Chapter - 51

"Are you sure…?" asked Shreya.
"Yes, I am…"
"But what if you break your hand or something, think about your husband. You have a life you need it, I will do it…" said Riya.
"No… I will and don't argue with me on this".
''But what about your husband… if something went wrong…? You could lose your hand… forever".
"Yeah she is right …? Maya, think about it…" said Ravi.
"NO!... you won't do it…" said Shreya.
Mayank also warned her butin middle he got interrupted by a burst out of Maya.

"I don't have husband…. Not anymore!!" she screamed and her eyes got wet, the secret she was holding for so long, was out now. She just couldn't lie anymore; the past pain and the present pain got together and broke her.
For a moment or maybe longer, there was only silence. No

one said a word not even for condolence, maybe they were too shocked to react, or maybe they couldn't figure out what to say, anyway. Again there was silence but also this time it was different from all the other times, this time it had pain and suffering of a girl, realization of friends (what they had been saying to her and teasing her, about her husband, since the moment they had met), it had anger in it for doing so with regret and guilt, these three always go together. They have a pretty good bond of whatever they have: Love or friendship or any other relation, but it's very strong, indeed.

"Say… something. Don't go silent on me…!" said Maya, crying with tears.
"What!!!... What happened…? How…?" Mayank broke the silence.
"I am too stunned, to speak…" said Shreya.
"I am out of words… don't know what to say!" said Riya.
"Me too…" (Ravi)
"What happened… and when…?" "Why didn't you say something to us, you didn't say anything… why?"
"I am sorry… Maya, I am very sorry…" Shreya said, still consuming what she just got told.
"I am sorry to hear that…" said Ravi
"Are you alright?" asked Mayank with tears.
"Yeah… how are you my friend?" asked Riya.
"I am… I am fine…" "As I said, I will do it…" she said again. This time no one argued or said anything to her.
"How… do I do it?"
"Push your thumb downwards, you will know when it gets dislocated…" explained Ravi.

"Okay… I am doing it!" Maya said looking at all of their faces, they were still in too much shock to stop her or do anything, so they simply let her do it.

Despite so much psychological pain, she still didn't hesitate not for a moment, to do something this big. That shows the strength of her character, I think if she had gotten the chance to be a mother she would have been a great mother, maybe she will one day, who knows.

"Ahhhh…." With the sound of a crack and her scream, it was clear that either her thumb broke or got dislocated.
"What happened… are you alright?" asked Shreya holding her steady, she was losing her balance because of pain.
"Yeah… I a… I am … fine!" she gathered all her strength and said. Women are really, an incredible species of creatures; you can't predict what they are capable of, just by merely looking at one. Our soft, innocent Maya did something that even the bravest people couldn't have done.

The plan worked, Maya's pain didn't go in vain. She was successful in freeing herself and sneaked into the other room, there was a cupboard as Mayank had said. Fortunately for their luck, it wasn't locked, she opened it and saw only one thing strong enough to cut the chains, an axe with still blood on its blade. As usual, she tried to use her dominant to pick it up but couldn't because of pain, so with her left hand she picked it up, it was heavy for her one hand.

"Guys… look, I found it…"
"Good…"

"Is that blood…?" Riya said in shock.
"Yeah… maybe… let's free all of you!"
"But, how would you do it… with the left hand?"
"I don't know, Shreya… let's try,"
"I believe in you… you can do it, Maya" said Mayank.
"Thank you, Mayank… so are you guys ready?"
"Do it..!"
"Yes, we all believe in you…do it!"
"Go ahead… just don't cut my hand, it's my favorite hand…" said Ravi and laughed.
"Be ready Ravi… on three…1…2..."
"Wait… but why do I have to go first?"
"Because you are strongest of us all… aren't you?"
"Yeah… do it!" he said.
"On three…1…2…3" (BAM!!) the sound of axe hitting the ground and cutting something was loud.

Chapter - 52

"He is on the throne and they are… dancing around it?" said Riya.
"Yeah… they are dancing!"
"How do we free him…?" asked Mayank.
"We need a distraction… we can't free him in front of them," said Shreya looking at the people.
"I have an idea… do any of you have a lighter or matchbox?" Ravi inquired.
"Why…?"
"I am going to light a hut…"
"So… why do you need a lighter, Idiot! There are torches everywhere around us…!"
"Ohh… sorry… I forgot. On it…!"
"Run!!... We don't have much time. Let's free him…!" said Maya, as everyone from the village ran towards the fire. They got their chance to free him, strangely they hadn't tied him, he was just sitting on the throne, by his own will, but why?
"Hey… Sandeep… get up. We are here for you… hello… are

you even listening…?" asked Shreya.
"What the fuck…! I think he's not conscious..."
"But how…?" "His eyes are wide open and blinking… but he is not responding on anything like he cannot hear us or is unable to answer...!" said Riya, and snapped fingers in front of his face.
"He is under some influence… maybe he is hypnotized…!"
"What… how do we take him from here, then? We don't have much time…"
"We have to carry him…!" said Maya.
"Okay… you all run towards Forrest. I will carry him…" said Ravi. Indicating them to run.
"Let's go… guys! Run…!"

They all ran towards the forest and Ravi followed them with Sandeep on his shoulder. He didn't even resist, whatever shit he was on, it was strong. They found that hut in which they had stayed before getting abducted, but it was no longer safe, the people knew about it now. There was nothing else, no place to stay in the forest, so they kept running until they found themselves in a strange place with no trees at all, it was like a desert with mountains, the forest was behind them now.
"Where do we go now…?" asked Ravi.

"Look… there is something at top of the mountain. I think it's a place we should go there…!" said Shreya, pointing towards (what looked like an old Palace or Castle) as we see in Hollywood movies.
"Let's go then…"

Chapter - 53

It was not a palace but an abandoned temple of maybe some Ancient God, and yeah this time it was God because the place was made up of white marble and there were paintings on the ceiling, gold engraved pillars, and precious stones were still intact in the paintings. There were rubies, emeralds and diamonds, and many others, but the place was not clean, it looked like a haunted house. Spider webs were all over the place and rats running on the ground, lizards, and other insects were also enjoying their stay, there.

The idol in the middle of the temple was broken, like something heavy hit it, it was not clear whose it was. There was no head, only one hand had left and lower portion of the body, the belt on the waist had some writing on it but in some different language.

"I think we should take shelter here…!"
"What is this place…?" asked worried Riya.
"Maybe… it was once a temple, but now only a ruin…"
"Let's sit… I am tired!"

"Is it still hurt...?" asked Ravi.

"Yeah… but not much, I am not feeling pain anymore… strange but it was hurting like hell before..."

"Serious… nothing…?"

"No… not even, sting…" Maya said looking at her hand, strangely.

"There is no swelling... there should be... isn't it?" said Shreya.

"Yeah... there should be, but it looks fine..."

"I think... it is healing!!"

"But how is that possible?"

"I am not sure but maybe because of this place..."

"I think so too..." said Shreya, on the word of Riya.

"But how...?" asked Mayank.

"I don't know... but I feel powerful since I entered this place..."

"I too feel good... I was exhausted and hungry but not anymore!" said Ravi.

"Ahhhh....!!"

"What happened...Maya?" asked Riya and Shreya together.

"What...? Are you all right...?" asked Mayank.

"I think... my thumb just went back to its place...!" said Maya, still in pain from the bone recovering.

"How...?" asked shocked Ravi.

"I don't know... it just got healed!"

"See, if you can move it..."

"Yeah... I can and it doesn't hurt anymore..." said Maya in relief.

"It's magic...!" said Riya.

"I don't believe in magic...!" argued Shreya.

"So... then, how would you explain it...?" asked Mayank.

"I don't know but, still... I don't believe in magic!"

"It could be true..."

"Are you serious Riya...?"

"Yes, I am...I have read about it too... I think it is 'Ra' the sun God!"

"What Ra...?"

"The God of this temple, whose idol that was...!" said Riya, pointing towards it.

"What do you want to say?" inquired Maya.

"I have read that back in 16 or 17 century... people used to worship 'Ra', even in India, only in some parts... some tribes used to worship him..."

"Yeah so what... it was in the past?"

"Maybe, we are in the past...!" said Riya.

"How...?"

"I don't know Ravi, but I think somehow we traveled back in time, directly from school to here...!"

"I don't believe in all that shit... time-traveling...seriously?"

"Don't... it doesn't matter. I think it's the truth..." said Riya, and sat on the ground.

"Holy... Shit...!"

"Now what... we are stuck in a different time, in a strange place with people who wants to murder us. How do we go back now...?"

"I have no idea...!" replied Riya.

"Didn't you read... how to go back?"

"No... Shreya, I didn't...!"

"Since school time... you only read useless stuff..."

If you are so smart, you get us out of here..."

"I didn't say... I am,"

"Where I am...?" asked Sandeep, regaining consciousness.

"Hey look... he's up!"

"Yeah... we all can see that, Ravi...!" said Riya sarcastically.

"You are with us... and safe. Don't worry...!" said Mayank.
"But how did I get here...? I was... I don't remember!"
"It's a long story..." said Ravi.
"You guys have some... long stories!"
"Believe me... you really wouldn't want to know!" said Maya.
"The basic is... we are back in time and don't know how to go back..."
"What...?" asked shocked Sandeep.
"Yeah... it's true!"
"Don't forget we still have to go back to get the book. We can't leave it... here!"
"Are you crazy...? If we go back...We are dead...!"
"But, she is right... we have to get the book or more people will die...!" said Maya.
"I am not going back there... it's final!" said Riya.
"We don't have any other option... we don't have a choice," argued Shreya.
"Don't worry... I will go back and get the book!" said Mayank.
"I am with you..." said Maya.
"But we have to find a way to... go back".
"How... where are we going to find it...?" asked Ravi.
"We have to divide into two groups... I and Riya will stay here, you three go and get the book...!" said Shreya.
"What about me...?" asked Sandeep, confused.
"You stay here... they like you too much. We can't take you back there..."
"Yeah... Ravi is right, but why is he so important... special?" asked confused Maya.
"First do the task at hand... then we will think about that..." said Shreya.
"Let's go... best of luck!" said Mayank to Riya as they left.

Chapter - 54

"Look...guys, there is the book...!" said Mayank, pointing in one direction.
"But where is everyone...?" asked Maya.
"Does it matter...? Just get the book and let's go back..." said Ravi.
"No... Ravi, what if they attack us from behind...?"
"So... you stay here, keep watch. I and Mayank will get the book..."
"Okay, Go...!"
Mayank and Ravi ran towards the book, which was on a showcase, totally unguarded. As Ravi touched the book, he fell back from a shock; the book was not as unguarded as it was looking, there was a strange force field around it, invisible to eyes but can be felt.
"What is it...?" asked Ravi, shaking his hand in pain.
"I think... some kind of force field!"
"How do we get the book now...?"
"Can you move this stand...?"

"Yeah... I think. Force field is only around the book...not the stand."

"Then, let's take the whole stand along with the book..."

"Seriously...?" asked Ravi, looking strangely at him.

"Do you have any other idea...?"

"You get the top... I got the bottom. On... three!" said Ravi, bending down to pick it up.

"One... two... three... Up...Up...! Keep it steady!" said Mayank.

"I am trying... it's heavier than it looks...!" Ravi said, his face turning red because of the excessive weight.

"Let's go...!" said Mayank to Maya.

"What the hell...! Why did you take the whole stand?"

"We will tell you...when we reach there... just run!"

"We are here...!" said Mayank, catching his breath.

"Just put it down... I can't feel my shoulder..."

"Carefully...!" they put it down.

"What the hell... where is the book and what's this...?" Shreya inquired.

"Wait... let me breathe!" said Mayank.

"The book is it... in some kind of force field!" replied Maya.

"Where...?"

"In here..." she said, pointing a finger.

"You guys took the whole stand..." Riya said and laughed.

"There was no other way... we couldn't think of anything else..." said Mayank still breathing heavy.

"You guys did well..." Shreya said and laughed.

"How do we get it out...?" asked Sandeep, looking at it from every corner.

"I have no idea..." said Shreya.

"What did you guys find...?"

"Not much...just that those people used to worship here but then something happened, that changed their faith in him... they just, stopped praying here..." said Riya.

"What happened...?"

"We have no idea...!"

"Just this... nothing about going back... home!" said Ravi, getting frustrated.

"No... Nothing about that!" said Shreya.

"There was no way to find out... we looked everywhere," said Riya.

Chapter - 55

"What is it....?" asked shocked Riya.
"I think it's fire.... The temple is on fire...!" said Ravi.
"What ...!"
"Its tribe people... they are trying to burn us!" screamed Mayank.
"What do we do now...?" "We need to get out of here!" Maya said, coughing in smoke.
"How the hell is this burning so fast...?"
"I think they have some kind of accelerant!" said Shreya, looking out from the window near the idol.
"We can't get out... they have surrounded us...!"
"And the air is non-breathable now... we have to get out or we will burn to crisp in a few minutes," said Riya, breathing heavily. The smoke had surrounded them by now, there was no place to hide or to leave, soon they will be burned alive.
"I can't breathe...khkhkhh..." said coughing Maya.
"Try to breathe slowly..." said Riya.
"Lie down on the ground... the air will be safer there"

indicated Shreya, pointing to the ground.

"I can't breathe... too!" said Sandeep, his face was black now because of smoke.

"Who are you...?" asked Ravi, shockingly.

"What... I am Sandeep!"

"Ohh... sorry!" he said, wiping his face.

"Seriously...Ravi... now!"

"What... I couldn't recognize him, his face was all black... it's not my mistake!"

"There are only six of us... here, you idiot!" screamed Shreya.

"Leave it guys... the heat is getting unbearable... we have to leave!!" said Mayank removing his coat.

"He is right... we have to get out or, it's over!"

"But, we can't... Riya, they are waiting for us outside... as soon as we got out, they will kill us...!"

"It's still better than being burned alive..."

"Watch out...!"

"Ahh..." "Thank... you, Mayank..." said Riya, she was just about to get crushed under a pillar that fell.

"The place is falling apart... we don't have time. What did you people decide...?" asked Ravi.

"We should leave...!"

"All right... so be it" .

"First I will get ou.....ahhhh!"

"What happened... are you all right? Ravi..."

"I am fine... guys!" Ravi screamed from a hole.

"What is that place..." asked Shreya.

"I think... it's a secret chamber under the idol, because of heat it moved and I fell!" he screamed again from there.

"Is it safe there....?" asked Riya.

"Yeah... I think... come down, you all..."

"Okay… let's move guys…move!"

"Move… Move…!"

"After you, Maya…"

"Sandeep… move faster!"

"Come faster… Mayank…!" Shreya screamed.

"I am coming…ahhh…" he screamed in pain.

"What happened… is he alright?" inquired Ravi, worriedly.

"I don't know… I can't see clearly. There is too much smoke…" replied Riya.

"Let me see…" said Ravi and pushed her aside.

"Mayank…brother…are you there…Mayank?"

"There is no one... up there… wait someone is coming…!!"

"What is it…? Ravi, What do you see…?"

"I saw one of those tribe men… I think they got him…!" he said, his face turned pale.

Chapter - 56

After they almost got burned alive, what they had fallen into was an old sealed chamber, that was sealed before even the temple was built as it had written on its wall 'Omayun' chamber sealed in the year 1669 and building of a temple of Sun god 'Ra', started in the year 1685. It was made 16 years after the chamber was sealed, those two dates and information were written in different styles, indicating being written by different people.

"We have to go back… for Mayank!"
"Yes…let's find a way to get out of here".
"Fast guys… he is in danger!"
"What is this place…?" asked Riya.
"I think it was a chamber where the book was sealed before these people found it and took it…" said Shreya.
"Who locked it here…?" asked Ravi.
"I don't know, but they were not… these people," said Shreya.
"Leave it guys… we have to save Mayank, it's a locked

chamber… how would we go out?" said Maya, panicking.
"There is no way out… it was designed to be only open from above," said Riya.
"Brilliant… first insane people… then fire and now this…! We are going to die…" said Ravi, sitting down on the floor.
"What the hell…!!" "Can't someone stay here safely… what is this place…" said Ravi in anger, he almost fell into another hole when he sat but got saved by Shreya.
"What is happening…?"
"I think it's… earthquake!!" said Riya.
"No… the ground is collapsing…!" screamed Shreya.
"What the hellllll……aahhhhh…!!!" screamed Riya, as they fell into a deep void.

Chapter - 57

"What do you think, Tavde… should we try to go into school again?"
"I don't think so, sir…"
"So how do we go back, then…?"
"I can't think of something... sorry, sir..." Tavde said, holding his head between his hands, he was so tensed. After Anand saw the man coming towards them, with his cut head in hand, they fell unconscious, when we woke up, they were still in school and there was no one around them, they came back to their room with a mild headache.
"I think we have to go back..."
"But why... after what happened last time... I don't think it would be a good idea".
"We have no other... choice, Tavde... we need to go back. We have to find a way back home!"
"You are right, sir... I think we should go back...!" he said, though one could see the fear on his face.
"We will go tonight... be ready!"

That night they again went to school, but this time with more safety precautions, like with a cricket bat and hockey. To their bad luck, there was a cult meeting going on at school, and they unwillingly became a part of it. At the back of the school, on the ground people were sitting on chairs, Anand counted they were five, for a change they were not wearing robes this time, though their faces were still hard to see in the dark.

"What are they doing, sir...?"
"I don't understand... I think there is a meeting going on," he said, looking from behind a tree.
"So... what should we do now?"
"I guess... we wait!"
"We should go nearto hear... what they are talking about..." said Anand.
"I think we should go back and come again...another time!"
"No... Tavde, we have to listen to what they are talking about"
"Come... we are going near..." Anand said and moved ahead towards the canteen, they took cover behind it.
"How long would we have to wait...?" asked one person.
"Till another, full blood moon...!" replied another one.
"How many years, are we talking about...?" asked the third person.
"Maybe... 10 years".
"10 years... shit!" "Why do we need to wait so long...?"
"It's not up to us... according to the calendar of the Cult... there will be no other full blood moon, till next 10 years..."
"So... what do we do, till then...?"
"We wait..."
"Okay... if that's what the new God wants... then, so be it!"

"How... will we contact each other again... when the right time comes?"
"We will know... don't worry?"
"So... there will be no contact between us, from now on, till the time comes. The Cult is dead now... understood?"
"Got it..."
"Okay..."
"Understood..."
"Hail... Satan!!"
"Hail... Satan...!" everyone said in unison.

"Isn't he Sandeep's father...?" asked said, looking at a man from the group.
"Yes sir... he is him!"
"So... he was a part of it, too..."
"Maybe... sir, Sandeep is also a part of this group..."
"He could be... Tavde... he could be".
"We should stop him...sir!"
"No Tavde... we can't. Don't you remember...?"
"Ohh... sorry, that time thing..."

Chapter - 58

They took pictures of them; fortunately, they still had some battery left in their phone. Even though in these situations, the battery of the phone always dies in T.V. shows and movies, didn't happen in real. After they all left school, Anand and Tavde...went into the canteen, but that creature was not there again this time, so the school building became their next stop, they searched every floor and every classroom but there was nothing, no ghosts nothing at all. The place looked normal like even the ghosts were afraid of those Cult people.

But as they were going to leave, they heard the crying of a woman, she started slowly but then she was crying manically, screaming and shouting were also a part of that. They followed it, in the principal office a woman was sitting on the table with her back towards the door, the door was unlocked and it wasn't broken. As they walked further, her sound of crying became unbearable, their ears started bleeding and they lost balance, finally falling to the ground.

The woman stopped crying and turned towards them, to their horror she was wearing that robe like those cult people, and in her hand was Anand's head and near her was Tavde's, body parts were spread all over the table, she was cleaning Anand's head with a corner of her robe, then she put it in front of her and his eyes met Anand's, Anand was looking right straight into the eyes of the head (which also looked like him), the head spoke...

"Why did you come here...? See what you have done. It all happened because of you, look now only my head is left... they ate the rest... it happened because of you. You shouldn't have come here... you bastardddd!!" the head screamed. "Because of you Vishal died... and now, Tavde will too... all because of you. You are a stroke of bad luck to anyone, who comes near you, dies....!"

"Now it's your time...to die!!!" screamed the head of Tavde, it was on a chair which turned towards them.

"What... what is it, sir...?" asked Tavde, crying like a kid.
"Keep it together, Tavde... we need to stay alive!"
"I am afraid... and, who is Vishal. What is it talking about?"
"He was my brother... he died when I was a kid."
"What... how?"
"It doesn't matter... Tavde, let's get out..."
"My head is spinning... I can't walk!"
"Come... take my hand"
"Ahhh..." Tavde screamed, the crying got so loud, blood started coming out of their eyes.

"Tavde... get up... are you alright?" Anand said shaking his body, which was lying on the ground like a dead duck.
"Stop!!!" "Just fucking stop!!" Anand screamed.
"I didn't kill him... he didn't die because of me!!"
"Yes, of course... he died because of you... you killed him" the head said with a maniac laugh.

He too fell right beside Tavde, as he lost consciousness he saw Vishal standing there next to the head, saying: "You did that... you killed me, you could have saved me that day...if you had just waited...", "Yes... you are right, it was me... I am so sorry my brother... I am so sorry. I was your big brother, I was supposed to keep you safe but I didn't... I am nothing but a failure... Please forgive me Visha..." Anand said, and then he passed out.

Chapter - 59

"Wake up sir... wake up...!"
"Huh... what happened Tavde... where are we...?"
"We are at school... sir," "I think we are back in our time..." Tavde said as he looked around at the school building.
"What...! Really, are we back?"
"Yes Sir, we are..." and they both smiled at each other.
"Where were you Anand...?" asked the Commissioner.
"I was underground Sir... Me and Tavde, for the school case..."
"Ohh... okay, I see... so what you got?"
"We found some serious clues that might end this investigation for good..."
"Really...! That's good, what did you find exactly...?"
"Sir... we found the people who may be involved in Sandeep's disappearing and also in one of the old cases of the 2000s, about children kidnapping from that same school..." "I think these two cases are somehow... related!" Anand said, with a smile.
"Ohh... that's brilliant, I mean that's good news not only for

the police department but for you too...!"

"I hope so...sir!"

"Well done, Anand... you may go now".

"Okay, Sir...Jay Hind" he said and gave a salute.

"Wait... Anand...!"

"Yes, Sir..."

"I was thinking, it would be good, not to dig up an old case... just finish yours".

"But, Sir... would it not be good, if we close that case, too..."

"There are people connected to that case...parents! Who might want closure and find out the truth behind the disappearance of their children..."

"Yeah... I know, that would be good but it's not your case... just leave it!"

"But Sir...!" he said trying to persuade him.

"No...Anand, as I said... leave it alone!" "Understand...?" Com. Said looking directly into his eyes and he was pretty serious this time.

"Okay...sir. As you say..." Anand said and left.

"Hello... commissioner speaking!" "I want to talk to you about something...Remember I told you about that inspector... Anand, it seems like he has a lead in your case... I have told him to stop but I doubt that he would..." "Hmm... I understand, okay, will take care of him. Don't worry..." he said, putting down the receiver.

"Constable...!!!!" he screamed from the cabin.

"Yes... sir!"

"I want you to give Raka... my message; I have a task for him... and tell him it's most important!"

"Okay, sir..." he said and left with a salute and a note written by Commissioner.

Chapter - 60

"I am going home..." "When Tavde... comes tomorrow tell him to report me, first thing in the morning," Anand said, leaving.

"Okay, Sir..."
It was night-time, around 11:00 pm; usually, he leaves early but because he had given Tavde, a day off, the workload was all on him from the past days. So he left late, got into the car, and took the shortcut to his home, as he was already late and didn't want to worry his mother further.

The shortcut was a road behind the highway, where usually nobody goes, so it remains empty. There was only his car, running fast on this empty road; suddenly a shot got fired at his windshield, just missing his right arm by inches. He lost the balance of the car but somehow managed to stop it, as he got out with a gun in his hand. He looked everywhere, but there was no one to be found, as far as he could see the road was empty with no street lights, it was only his car's light that was showing the road ahead.

There were some closed factories, on the left side of the road and trees on the right side. There was no one in sight, he searched the whole road and everything nearby but there was no proof of anyone else's presence, he got into the car and drove away.

"How are you, sir...?"
"I am good Tavde... how are you?"
"Good, Sir..."
"How's your wife...? Was she worried about you?"
"Yeah, she was a little... I think" he said looking confused.
"Good..." Anand said with a smile.
"What happened to your hand...?"
"Ohh, this... nothing, just an accident," Anand said looking at his arm, which was bandaged.
"It looks like you got shot... is that right?"
"Yeah... well, almost. You can say that..."
"What!!... What happened?"
"Last night I was on the factory road going home when somebody shot at me, but... his bad luck or my good luck, God knows... whoever it was missed me by inches!"
"Thank God... you are safe!" Tavde said, folding his hands in a praying gesture.
"Yeah"
"But what were you doing on that road, you don't take that road... why change?"
"Last night I got late and had to take that shortcut..."
"Ohh... so did you see anyone?"

"No... No one, I looked all around. Whoever it was either got out of sight pretty fast or it was a long shot.

"Did you find the bullet...?"

"No... It was dark and I was late, I didn't look for it..."

"We should go... look for it, Sir... it will help us in determining from which gun it got shot?"

"You think...?"

"Yes, Sir... we should look for it. It could be someone from the case we are working on... trying to stop you, as we are close to catching them!"

Chapter - 61

"Is it the place, where you got shot…?"
"Yes, this is it…"
"Let's search for the bullet...!"
"Here it is sir… I found it!" screamcd Tavde in excitement.
"Very good… let me see!"
"So, what do you think sir…?"
"It's a handgun bullet, it means whoever it was… was nearby," Anand said, looking at the bullet from all angles.
"Should we search for the weapon…?"
"No benefit… Tavde, we won't find anything. Whoever it was, was an expert in his field… the angle was perfect, if he hadn't missed I would have died, right there. That's what I don't understand, how did he miss…?"
"Maybe… he wasn't as expert as we thought, he was…"
"No… Tavde, something else happened… that we don't know!"
"Whatever happened…I am glad he missed!"
"Yeah…Lucky me!" Anand said, thinking.

"Who knew… you were going to take this road?"

"Nobody…Tavde"

"But somebody knew… definitely!"

"Yes… you are right" "Wait…!"

"What, sir… did you remember something?"

"Yeah… only commissioner sir knew about how close we have got to solve the case, I just told him yesterday and then this happened…"

"What do you mean…?" Tavde asked, confused.

"I think… I don't know. I could be wrong… but…"

"You think it was…!" Tavde said, shocked.

"Yeah… it could be…"

"Ohh…, my God!!!" "What do we do now…?"

"I don't know… Tavde, but one thing we know for sure, we can't trust anyone!"

"Holy, shit!!" "I never could have thought… Police Com.!"

"Neither could I… Tavde" Anand said, looking worried.

"Let's go back to the police station…"

"Okay…sir"

"You wanted to meet me…Sir?" Tavde said as he stepped outside the vehicle at the police station.

"Yes… I need you to find those people we saw; I need our every resource on it… I want every detail about them; they are alive or dead doesn't matter…" "Tavde… this case is our No.1 priority…"

Chapter - 62

"Sir…!"

"Yes, Tavde…"

"I got some information…"

"Tell me…go ahead…"

"As we know out of five, one is already dead…Sandeep's father and the remaining four are still alive… but you won't be happy to know, who they are…" he said looking at a file in his hand.

"Go on… tell me!"

"(With a deep sigh, He said…) one of them is an army officer at High Rank, another one is a minister of Jharkhand and the third one is a businessman!"

"What about the fourth…?" Anand asked closing file which was in front of him.

"That's the main concern… the fourth one is our Police Commissioner 'Amit Gaotonde!'…" he said, looking worried and scared.

"FUCK!!!" Anand said and hit the table. "That's what I was

afraid about…!"
"So… what now, Sir…"
"Now… we have to be careful"
"Okay…"
"Tell our informers to keep an eye on them…"
"Yes, sir…"

"When is the full blood moon, I think it's been 10 years… it's the time!" "Find out when is it… they are going to come back to their crime spot…We need to be there for their welcome...!"
"Okay sir, will do…" he saluted and left.
"Commissioner is with those people… Shit! That makes the work harder" (Anand was thinking) "Let's pay him a visit…"
"May I come in, sir…?"
"Yes… come" he said, while looking at a file, and didn't see him.
"Sir…!"
"Yes… what is it?" he said, head still down.
"Nothing…sir, just monthly case reports," Anand said, with a file in his hand.
"Yes… what were you…, Ohh Anand! It's you…" Com. said, with a disappointed face.
"Sir… file!"
"Ohh…yes, give it to me…" he said and took the file.
"Can I go now…?"
"Yes… please!"
"And sir, sorry I forgot to tell you… I was wrong about the info on the child kidnapping case, it was wrong Intel … we still haven't got anything"
"Is it…! Are you sure?" his face lit up.
"Yes, sir… the information turned out to be wrong," Anand

said with a sad face.

"Don't worry, Anand… it happens. Don't be sad…!"

"(sigh) Yes sir… this time I thought, we got them…but now I will be focusing on the present case, rather than the closed one…"

"Very good, decision… Anand!"

"I should go now, Sir…" he asked politely.

"Sure!" Com. said with a smile and Anand left.

Chapter - 63

"Sir…!"

"Yes, Tavde… what is it? You look happy!"

"The blood moon is very soon, it's this year… even this very month!" he said with a smile.

"When is it…? Tell me!!

"It's next week sir, on Friday…!"

"That's brilliant…! Well done, Tavde…" "Just keep it to us, for now…"

"Okay, sir… don't worry".

"And yeah, Tavde… I told the Com. I am dropping that child disappearing case…"

"What!! Are we…?" he asked shocked.

"Of course not… it was to keep him off, our backs," he said with a smile.

"That's a very good idea, sir…! You are very smart…!"

"Thank you… Tavde, just keep it between us, understood!"

"Yes, sir…"

"And be ready…! It's time for us to catch, some criminals…!"

"I will…sir".

"Sir… I got information that a body has been found…at where

you got shot".

"Who is it…?"

"It's… Raka, sir"

"How did he die…?"

"He was strangled… by some wire!"

"What was he doing there…?" Anand asked surprised.

"That we don't know…" "But I think… he was the one who shot you!"

"That could be possible, Tavde… but the question is, who killed him?" Anand said, confused.

"And another question…! Who sent him…?"

"That… I think we know, that answer…"

"You…think he did!"

"Either he or someone, he knows…"

"You can't even trust your department…! How will people trust us, to keep them safe… when we are not safe, ourselves?"

"It is bad… Tavde, but we will bring them to justice… they will get punished!"

"Would we…?"

"Definitely…! We will. You don't worry… just be careful!"

"Yes, sir"

"I don't understand…one thing; Raka is a trained shooter… how he missed!"

"Maybe…Sir, whoever killed him… got him at the time he was going to shoot you…"

"Yeah… I think that too… whoever it was, he or she saved my life…"

"You think… It could have been a girl?"

"I don't know…Tavde, but one thing I have learned from this job is…anything could be possible!"

"Hmmm…"

Chapter - 64

"Wake up guys!!!"

"Huh… where I am?" Ravi said getting up.

"We are home…!"

"What…! How did we get here…? I remember falling in the temple…"

"Yes… we did, and somehow we are back…!"

"Where are we…?"

"At school…where we left!"

"Wake up… Riya… Maya…!"

"What happened to Mayank… where is he…?" Maya said, looking around.

"I don't think so; he made it…" Shreya answered.

"What!!! No…!!! No…no…no…, that can't be true?"

"Calm down! Maya…, keep yourself together…!"

"How the hell, did that happen…!!!!" Ravi said, with tears.

"It's bad, guys… it's bad!" Riya said, holding her head between both hands.

"What are we gonna tell… to his family?"

"I don't know… I have no idea!" Shreya said.

"We shouldn't have gotten into this case, in the first place…! It's all our doing!" said Maya, now crying with tears.

"It's not our doing Maya… don't blame yourself. He was in it, on his own will…"

"No! We did that... we are to blame for it!"

"No... We aren't" screamed Riya.

"NO! Maya is right... we did it" said Ravi.

"What do we do now?"

"I don't know...!" Shreya said.

"We have to finish... what we started".

"Are you out of your mind...? Riya!"

"No...I am not, Maya. But that book...where is that book?"

"I think we lost it in the temple...!"

"WHAT!!! Total waste of time... after all this trouble, we couldn't bring the book and also we lost our friend..."

"Shit!!" "We really need that book; I think that book can bring back Mayank!"

"What...!... How...!"

"That I don't know, Maya...but I think there is still a chance to bring Mayank back, but we need that book..." "We have to finish...what we started, now more than ever..."

"But how the hell are we going to get that book... it's in past and we can't go back on our own..."

"We don't need to go back...Ravi," said Shreya.

"What! What do you mean by that?"

"The book is already here...people involved with Mansukh uncle, definitely have that book... we can still get it!"

"Ohh...Yes! It's here..."

"We should immediately go to Sandeep's house..."

"Wait... a minute...!! Where the hell is Sandeep...? He was

with us when we fell...!"

"Yeah... because of Mayank, we totally forgot about him...!" said Riya.

"Yes... where is he?" asked Ravi, looking around them.

"Maybe, he is somewhere in the school...! We should find him... let's go".

"Okay... I and Riya will search... here, you two search in the school...okay!"

"I am not going...in there!"

"Don't worry, Ravi... its day time. You will be fine...!"

"Yes... let's go, Ravi..." said Maya.

"Okay..."

Chapter - 65

"Wake up! Sandeep... wake up!" shouted Shreya.
"We need water...to sprinkle!"
"Ravi!!!!... Maya!!!! Come here, we found him, and bring some water with you..." Riya shouted.
"What!!"
"Here he is... did you bring water?"
"Here... take it".
"What is it... why it is in your shoe?"
"What! We couldn't find anything else... just do it!" Ravi said.
"Wake up! Sandeep..." Shreya said and sprinkled water.
"Huh... who am I... who are you?"
"Sandeep!!!" screamed Maya.
"Oh... yeah I remember now, but where are we...?" he asked getting up from the ground.
"We are at school...!"
"What! Back in our time...?"
"Yes... you are home!"
"I can't believe... I thought I would never see my family again.

I thought I lost them forever...My mother! My wife...!"
"Let's go... I want to meet my family".
"Yeah..."
"Wait! Where is your other friend... the short, thin one...?"
"His name is Mayank...!" shouted Maya in anger.
"Shh...Calm down, Maya" "He couldn't make it...back with us", Shreya said, looking down.
"What!!!" Sandeep said in shock.
"Yes..."
"I am so sorry... you all saved me, but we lost him... I wish there was a way to bring him back".
"There is...!"
"What! How...?"
"Stop... Riya, don't tell him... did you forget, what we decided?"
"Let her tell him... Ravi, it doesn't matter anymore... we can't save him from the truth, forever..."
"What!! But it was your idea too... not to tell him! Maya..."
"Yeah... I know! But it doesn't matter anymore... for Mayank, he needs to know the truth..."
"Yeah... she is right! Ravi".
"Okay... go on!" said Ravi, holding up his hands in the air.
"What! What are you saying... that can't be true?"
"It's true... son," said his mother, crying and hugging him again and again but he didn't let her touch him anymore.
"What! Why...?" he said, sitting down.
"Your father said... he will give us everything, we wanted..."
"And you did that...! Ma!" "How could you? Do that!"
"I didn't... your father did!"
"Yeah... but you helped him! How could you...?"

“Pack our bags... Sangeeta! We are leaving this house...now!”
“What! What are you saying son... where will you go? Don’t leave me alone... I don’t have anyone else, but you...” mother said, crying with sound now.
“I will live on the road! but I will never live with, murderers!!!”
“Don’t... don’t say that...Son! Please!!”
“No... You are not my mother... not anymore! You are a murderer’s accomplice...”
“Please!!! Don’t say that son... you are my son! I am your mother...” she said while holding his face.
“We are going! And that’s final... pack our bags...Sangeeta!!”
“Tujhe meri Kasam!!! You will not go...” she said, swearing at him.
“Aunty... we need that book!” said Shreya, stopping their drama.

Chapter - 66

"When is the 'blood moon' ...?" asked Ravi.
"I checked on Google... it's next week!" replied Shreya.
"Next week!!!" said Riya in shock.
"Yes..."
"That's when they are going to meet...right?" asked Maya.
"That's what Aunty said...!"
"Then we will be waiting for them..." said Shreya.
"Let's buckle up guys... it's time for the showdown!"
"I am ready!!" said Ravi.
"Me too!" said Riya.
"Let's bring our friend back and... bring some criminals to justice!" said Maya.
"We need to gather some things...!"
"Like what!"
"We may have to fight them... we need to be ready!"
"We should go and tell the police...!"
"Who will believe us...?"
"I don't know... but we can't take law into our own hands... we need to inform the police..."

"Who was the inspector of Sandeep's case; we should talk to him…"

"Yeah, Ravi is right! He would be able to understand…"

"How would we find out who was the inspector in charge…?" said Riya.

"We should ask Aunty…!" said Maya.

"Yeah, that could work…"

"So… we will go there again tomorrow".

"Why is the phone ringing…? Who would call us here?"

"Nobody knows we are here… not even our families, and even if they were calling, that would be on mobile, not landline!" said Shreya.

"Just pick up the phone!"

"Hello… who is this?" asked Ravi, picking up the phone.

"Room no. 102…?" said a voice on phone.

"Yes… who are you?"

"I am calling from reception… police are here to meet 'Ravi, Maya, Riya, Shreya, and Mayank, do you know these people…?"

"Yes…I am Ravi, and others are my friend's names" "Who is it… you say wants to meet us?"

"Police…! They want to meet all of you…so please come to the reception…Thank you!" said the person on phone hanging up.

"Who was it…?" asked Shreya.

"Police… he said they want to meet us!" Ravi replied.

"What…! Police! Why…?"

"How would I know…?"

"Come on… let's see for ourselves, what is the matter…!"

"It's strange… we wanted to go to the police. Police came to us, instead…" said Ravi.

"Yeah… Come!" said Maya, walking out of the door.

"Are you Ravi…?" asked the police officer.

"Yes… I am!"

"And these are Maya…Shreya…and Riya?"

"Yes…they are!"

"Where is Mayank…?"

"He… he is… he…"

"He went home…!" said Shreya, from behind.

"When…?"

"Yesterday…!" said Riya.

"Did you know about it…?"

"No… I didn't" replied the Manager.

"We were going to tell him, we were out so couldn't…!" said Ravi.

"Can I ask… what is this about, Inspector?" Shreya asked before he could ask more about Mayank.

"Yes…! I want to ask you about…Sandeep! Last night, he returned home… on his own. We asked him, where he was and he said he was with you guys… then he told some strange story…!"

"Can we talk in private, Sir…?" asked Ravi.

"Sure…!" "So… tell me, was he with you?" asked the Officer, sitting on a chair.

"Yeah… that's why we wanted to talkin the room!" said Ravi.

"What he told you was true…" Shreya said.

"What…!"

"Yes…it's the truth!" said Riya.

"So… let me understand, you are saying… you all traveled back in time and there you meet Sandeep, who was already there…! And then you brought him back with you…?"

"Yes… that's the full story, Officer"

"I know… you won't believe us, but it is true!" said Maya.

"Well... I do believe you!" Anand said, they all looked at him in shock.

Chapter - 67

"Tavde…! You won't believe what happened…?"
"What happened…Sir?"
"Some people also traveled back in time like us…!"
"What…! Who…?"
"You remember five people that disappeared from school…?"
"Yes… I do!"
"Those people returned yesterday… and guess what! With Sandeep…!"
"So they… traveled back in time? Just like us!"
"Yes… they did!" "And Sandeep met them, where they were gone… in time!"
"So… where did they go?"
"According to them… they went a lot further than us, to Sixteenth Century…!"
"Ohh, God! Sixteenth-century!"
"Yeah…Tavde"
"So…Sandeep is back, safe and sound?"
"Yes…but, they all didn't return safely!"

"What!"

"Yeah… one of the five people, Mayank, went with them but couldn't come back!" Anand said with a sad face.

"What happened…?"

"Long story but the point is he didn't come back… and now they want our help to catch the culprits and somehow bring their friend back…"

"How would they get him back?"

"They were talking about a book… they think, that can bring him back!"

"What book?"

"I don't exactly know about that… but I am gonna help them!"

"Why, sir…?"

"Because they know more about this case than us, and they told me some things that were also true…" "They even showed me… a pendant that was supposed to be from that century… I don't know Tavde, but this case… it's much bigger than we thought".

"Yes, sir… It's not one of our usual cases…definitely!"

"What do we do now, sir…?"

"We wait for the blood moon…!"

"That's all we can do, for now…" Anand said, sitting on his chair. "We have to be ready… for the blood moon, Tavde… it's going to be the biggest 'Case' of our careers!"

"Should we tell anyone else…?"

"No…Tavde! We can't… even if we caught them, still we can't bring them here…"

"So… what would we do with them…?"

"We will bring them to justice… some other way. I have an idea for that…" Anand said with a smirk.

THE DAY

"Today is the day…!"
"Yeah… I remember" said Ravi.
"If one of us or all of us dies today… in that case, we should call our families," Shreya said.
"Do you think we are going to die…?" asked Ravi.
"I don't know but just in case… we have to be ready for everything!"
"She is right… we have already lost Mayank! We should talk to our families… maybe, it would be our last talk with them…"
"Don't say that… we haven't lost Mayank!" said Mayain anger.
"I meant… we almost lost him!" Riya said, trying to calm her.
"Hmm…" said Maya.
"I am going to call my mother…" said Ravi, going out of the room.
"Me too…" said Shreya.
"I should call my parents too, hasn't talked to them… it's been a while…" said Maya, also leaving the room.

Riya was left alone in the room. She had no one left to talk to, no one will remember her if she died tonight. She had no parents, no friends other than those, whom she was with already. She left the room too, so she would not feel alone or left out. As she walked out towards the exit, Ravi was talking on his phone in the corridor; Maya was outside in the cafeteria. Shreya was standing under a tree outside the exit gate, talking on the phone. She left them all for a while, they needed their privacy and she needed hers. There was silence outside on the road like people didn't want to go out on blood moon, as it was some sort of bad omen, only her mind was not silent, it was rhyming with thoughts, she was thinking, she should call someone but, who? She couldn't figure out that.

She kept walking until, it was a dead-end, there was no one around, so she sat on the bricks, lying there probably from someone's house construction. All alone at the end of the road, it felt like it was the end of her story, she wasn't able to keep her mind calm, she knew she had to.

She thought of her parents, her father before he left them, and her mother lying on her deathbed, waiting for death. Then suddenly her mind went to thinking of Saranshand his parents, obsessive and overprotective but still at least he had parents. Maybe they were not overprotective, maybe they just care for him too much because they love him too much, maybe that's how normal parents were supposed to be and she knew nothing about normal parents. It didn't mean her parents weren't good enough, they were but they were not normal, not from her point of view, her mother was too much husband devote, and her father was just not there for her. They provided her the best education and every luxury, a child could think of and she had a wonderful childhood, but something was missing… their presence in it.

She immediately took her phone out and called Saransh's parents, they were the closest to a family, she had left. She talked to his mother, who was asking when she will be back for tuition. She had told them that she would be gone for only two days but the period exceeded. She told her that she will be back soon and apologized for her delay, asked her how Saransh was and told her that he is a good boy, don't be so hard on him, he will learn his ways, he is smart, he will be just fine, they don't have to worry about anything. Let him live life a little and make sure to be with him in it. Tell him you love him and make him feel that he is important, that he matters in your life. Spend as much time with him as you could, as this time will never come back, and he needs them now, more than ever. So he could remember them when he gets old. She didn't talk about her, well; what was there to talk about.

As she ended the call she realized, she is not as alone as she thought, she had their memories. That was more than enough for now.

Shreya talked to her parents after a long time since that incident. They were nice people always there for her, always loved her, and took care of her every need. But as she grew up, she started to stay away from them, it wasn't that she did not love them anymore, she did, but as you grow up you somehow get apart from your parents, don't know why, but it was like that for her too. She used to call them but since the accident, she just confided in herself and stopped calling, she didn't want to hear their talk which was all about getting married, she was in no mood of getting married, anywhere soon, and they didn't want to talk about his dead boyfriend, for them it was only a timely affair which got over and now she had to move on. Nobody understood her feelings, her pain, her newfound loneliness; they just couldn't seem to grasp this concept, like it was out of their syllabus.

They were good parents, but not in the department of their daughter's love life, they just wanted her to get married and settle down. She needed someone to hear her cries at midnight, she needed someone's shoulder to put her head on, she needed someone to hold her hand through the night, she had her friend cum roommate but, she was also busy in her relationship as he proposed and she said 'Yes'. They were going to get married soon, so she didn't want to spoil her happiness by talking to her about a dead boyfriend.

Still, they asked her about how she was and told her to get over it, as death is a part of life and she couldn't do anything to save him. They still had no sympathy for her. So after talking to them, and saying them 'Love you' and 'Good bye', in a way that they would not understand the meaning behind it but would still take it. She finally got the courage to call her best friend, Anjali.

"Hello…Anjali…!"
"Why are calling, now…?" she asked.
"I just wanted to talk to my best friend…"
"What best friend…! The one who you left without even saying goodbye…"
"I am so sorry for that… I am, really sorry!"
"I don't want your sorry…!"

"Please... forgive me, Anjali. I was so wrong about not informing you... I did a mistake!"

"You did, what you did... why are you calling now?"

"I just wanted to talk to you... to tell you, how sorry I am...!"

"You have anything else to say? I am hanging up!"

"No! No ... please don't hang up on me...!"

"It means you have nothing to say... fine, Goodbye!"

"No... please Anjali... don't hang up the call... it might be our last conversation!!!" she screamed at the end, with no intention of saying that. When she realized what she had said, it was already too late. The truth was out.

"What!!! What did you just say...?"

"Nothing... let's not talk about it!"

"Tell me... understand! What did you just say?" she said, forcing her.

"I... I..."

"Yeah, you what...!"

"I said... it could be our last conversation..."

"What! Why...!"

"Because..." she told her the entire story.

"What...! What are you saying! Let me understand...First!"

"You are saying that... today is something called blood moon, and you with your friends are going to have a ghostly encounter at your school...?"

"Yes... that's what I am saying. That's the truth..."

"Why are you doing this...? Just leave... Come back!"

"You know, I can't...!"

First, you left me without saying and now are saying that I would not even get to meet you for one last time... I won't even get to see you!"

"I am...Sorry".

And then she burst out in tears.

"I am so sorry…" Shreya said, also crying.

"I don't know… just come back!"

"I am sorry…I can't, my friend!"

"I don't know… just come back!"

"Please…Anjali, try to understand".

"I don't want to understand…!" "You understand…! I want my friend back!!!"

"I wish… I could do that but I can't. I wish I would have never left you without even saying 'Good Bye'…"

"I am sorry, too…" Anjali finally, broke down. "I am sorry… I overreacted, I should have understood… why you did, what you did…!" "After what happened to you…! It wasn't your mistake; I should have been a good friend… I am sorry!"

"No…No… it's not your mistake. Don't blame yourself…! You have been a good friend, best friend…!"

"No!!! I should have reacted in a better way; I got so busy with my engagement and all that…I forgot about you; I wasn't there for you when you needed me… I should have been!"

"Don't blame yourself… it wasn't any of us mistake. The circumstances were difficult and we just reacted to them… Just leave it!"

"I wish I had been better with you…!" Anjali said.

"Me too… but it doesn't matter anymore".

"Listen to me! You come home safe… you understand! Come back safe… or I will kill you myself!" "Come to me… so I could punish you, my way…!" Anjali said, sobbing.

"Okay… I will!" Shreya said, wiping off her tears with a smile and they both laughed.

- Maya talked to her parents and told them, that she would be returning to them after this reunion, that she has finally decided to move on and give her life another chance. They were very happy to hear that and couldn't wait for her to come back home. They told her that they both love her so much and that she takes care of herself, and asked her why was it taking so long.

She told them that before coming back home and starting her new life, she had to take care of some things first.

"I still miss you so much...don't think I have forgotten you because of what I just said to my parents. I would never do that to you...I said that, well; you know why...Right!" Maya was talking to her husband's picture.

- Ravi called her mother, who scolded him for staying too long at the Reunion, she said him to come back now. Then she told her that she love him, so much, they both does and even his father has talked to one of his friends, and he got him a job as a basketball coach, she said she knows how much he loves it, that it was what he wanted to do in his life, but that stupid accident ruined everything. She told him, she had seen him crying alone in his room at night, looking at photos of his college team days, and that it had been killing her too, but she couldn't do anything and that was killing her more.

But now everything has changed, he will be happy again in this job, he won't be able to play, still, but at least he could teach kids and could stay in the field. "I am so happy, maa..." he said with teary eyes, he was trying hard to control the change in his voice, because of crying. But after some time, hearing her voice over the phone, and realizing that it could be their last conversation, he just broke down.

"Ravi...! What is it, son...?" "Why are you crying...tell me? Lalla... what happened!" she asked, she used to call him Lalla, when he was little, but she hadn't called him by that name since he completed school, because he told her to stop, as he felt embarrassed, when she used to call him that in front of his college friends.

"Maa...! Maa... it's nothing ma!" "Don't worry... I am absolutely fine..." he said, wiping his tears.
"No...! Don't lie to me... I am your mother! Tell me, Lalla... what is it?"

"I am not lying, maa...it's true, and I am fine. I will be home soon... don't worry, I will meet you soon..." it's hard to lie to your mother, but it's even harder when you are crying.

"I know you are lying... but I won't force you if you don't want to tell. I have already given you a hard time since you lost your job and I am so sorry for that..." she said, crying.

"No...! Maa...Please don't say that...!" "I am not angry at you...! I could never be... I love you soo much...!" "I love you both...!"

"I know that... son! And your father also loves you..." "Come home, soon... I am waiting for you!"
"I will... Ma... I will...!" he said and hung up the call.

BLOOD MOON (PART-1)

"Here we are…!" said Ravi, stepping out of the car.
"Are you guys ready…!" asked Shreya.
"I am ready…" said Riya.
"Me too, said Maya, with a bat in her hand.
"Where did you get that…?" asked Ravi.
"On the way here…!" replied Maya.
"You should have got one, for all of us…yarr!"
"Why do you want it…? Your one punch would be enough to knock out anyone!"
"Ohhh yeah… that's true!" Ravi said, punching his hand.
"We won't need it…!" said Shreya.
"I know… but just in case!" said Maya.
"Where are the Police?" asked Riya.
"They are coming… I talk to inspector Anand, this morning".
"Good…"
"And who is that…!" asked Ravi, pointing towards a car, coming towards them.
"Maybe Police…!"
"No! Riya… Police don't travel in normal cars… it's Ciaz!" said Shreya, looking carefully at the car.
"It's a lady…" said Maya, as someone came out of the car.
"Hello…" the lady said.
"Hello"
"Hi…"

"Hello…"

"Who are you…?" inquired Shreya.

"Shreya…! Where are your manners?" "Say hello to the lady!" said Maya, staring at her like a mother.

"Okay…okay… sorry!" "Hello there…!"

"Sorry… I should have introduced myself first!" "I am Manisha…Manisha Roy…"

"What!!!"

"What the hell!"

"I… we thought, you left!" said Riya.

"I did… but I was waiting for this day for a very long time…!"

"You knew, what is today…?"

"Yeah… it's blood moon! I waited for this…" "I had to finish, what I started…"

"So… you are here for the same thing, like us!"

"I don't know… who are you, people?"

"We are…" Shreya told her the whole story, and how they got there.

"So it happened to you too, people…! You have been through a lot in past these days…"

"Yeah… we have!"

"I am sorry, for your friend…"

"Thank you…!" said Maya.

"You people are deep in this case, more than me…" "I only knew about the disappearances, nothing about the cult and all…!"

"I have been wanting to ask you this… since I first heard about you! May I?" said Riya.

"Sure…" said Manisha.

"Why did you leave and took your case back?"

"Yeah… I want to know that too!" said Ravi.

"Will you please, tell us...? If you are comfortable with that...!"

"Okay... I think it's time, I reveal the truth... about why I did that?" she said with a deep sigh. "I was going to testify when... I got the call from my father that, my little sister had been kidnapped... and if I talk about them, they will kill her!"

"We never talked to anyone about this... that day, I refused to testify, and soon we left our home and the city...! It got too difficult to live here, after that..." "I couldn't see myself in the eye after that, but there was nothing...I could do!" "I love my sister... I couldn't risk her life!" Manisha said, now sobbing.

"Ohh...so... did your sister return safely?"

"Yes... she returned home, unharmed...!" "And when we asked her... where she was, she just couldn't remember anything... just some visions, nothing else. To this day...she wakes up in the middle of the night, because of nightmares of those visions...!" Manisha said, in a low voice.

"What were those visions...?" asked Shreya.

"Just being tied up in a dark room... and people with masks over their faces, coming to see her from time to time like she was on some kind of display...!"

"Holy shit...!"

"What exactly...happened to her?" said Riya.

"No one knows... till this day, not even she, herself..."

"Now... that we know each other, I think we should tell her our plan...?" said Maya.

"What plan...?"

Shreya explained her plan; it was to go inside with the police not without them and then help the police to get proof, then in catching the criminals. Get their hands on the book as soon as possible, read it, and find a way to get Mayank back, as they knew that the book translates itself into the language of whoever's reading it. And if anything goes wrong, kill them all and get out of there, hopefully alive, not leaving anyone behind. The plan was safe, catch them if you can or finish them, and don't let them leave that place alive, that night. You probably would be thinking that that's murder and I am not going to give any justification because that is, wrong, but under these circumstances where they cannot take them into police custody, and these people were too dangerous to walk outside, it was the best choice to kill them. Anand had given them Green Light, in any case, things get out of hand, to save themselves and their friends. He knew this was against the law, but so was everything they had done, till now.

You cannot beat evil without getting your hands dirty, let's hope that they get dirty in mud, not blood.

BLOOD MOON (PART-2)

"Keep your voice down... doesn't make any noise!" Anand said, going inside school.
"Let's go...go...don't stop, keep going!" Ravi said.
"Be careful and stay safe...!" Riya stopped to tell, Ravi.
"You too..." he said and nodded.
"I am on it..." Riya said to Anand while leaving for the school rooftop.

"You two go there and Tavde... you come with me!" "And you know what to do!" Anand said looking at Ravi; they all had taken their place. Ravi was on the third floor; Shreya and Riya were hiding at parking spots behind school buses, Anand was on the roof of the canteen with Tavde, ready to shoot with rifles.

As the night came, the eclipse started turning the whole place pink because of the blood moon; it was like looking at a black and white T.V. with a pink screen. Everything was pink and with that came the members of Cult, in their red robes with hoods on their heads. Because of the red color, it was making hard to see any of their faces in the pink environment. The eclipse started exactly at 11:50 pm, Friday, they started doing preparations for their ritual.

There were seven people, there. One of them was chanting in some strange language, in front of something, but that was not visible from my side, as they were all surrounded by it. I was hiding in the children's playground, just near the door which leads to the ground.

Then they all bowed down in front of it, it was an idol of some strange creature, with a human body and head of a goat. One person brought some goats and chopped their head off, their blood splashed on the idol's face. Then one person drained their blood in a big bowl, which had something written on it, it looked like gold. I had never seen something like that before, it looked old but was still shining like new. Then he put the bowl in front of the idol, dipped his fingers in blood, and made something on his face, then on everyone else's. Then they all cut their hand one by one, drops of blood fell into the same bowl.

I looked at my watch it was striking exactly midnight. The moon had fully turned pink now; one person drew something on the ground with that blood, at the same time another man brought some people, their heads were covered like they do when they hang someone on the death penalty. Their hands were tied behind their back; they were barely walking. "Hell... they are children! Same children that got abducted", I saw their faces as they unmasked them, their faces were fully perfect, with no wounds, and didn't look like they got any beating, but they were barely able to stand, as they kneeled on the ground. It looked like they were under the influence of some drug, I wanted to run and beat the shit out of those people but I couldn't, at least not now. I saw the constable looking at them in anger, and the inspector calming him down.

Up on the roof was Maya, who almost jumped, seeing the children, she is so kind at heart, I think. Shreya and Riya were on the other side of the building, I couldn't see them. Ravi was also away from my sight. One of the cult members said something in another one's ear and he left the scene. Another person was speaking something, in every child's ear, one by one; totally inaudible from where I was standing. If they hadn't have kept holding their heads, those kids would have fallen to the ground by now.

That person came back with a big machete, dipped it in some kind of powder, and started sharpening it. A chill went down my spine, seeing that scene, I couldn't believe my eyes, they were going to murder those children. Soon one person brought that bowl near the children; he was forcing them to drink that blood. I almost puked. Children were unable to drink it on their own, so they opened their mouth and put a funnel in their mouth, through which one person poured the blood into their mouth. One by one all the children drank it and then puked, but it was in them now.

I was sick worried about what was going to happen, but suddenly something hit me on the head and I fell.

When I woke up, we all were in one of the classrooms, my eyes were still foggy. I saw Ravi, Shreya, Riya, and Maya tied up on the opposite side of the room on the right side were the inspector and constable, also tied up.

"What happened....?"

"How are you...?" Shreya asked.

"I am fine... just a little headache!" "What happened to us...?"

"We got caught... our plan was failed!" said Riya.

"What! How...?"

"They knew that we were there... even all of our hiding spots and our plan!"

"But how...?"

"Don't know!"

"What do we do now...?"

"I don't have a clue... Manisha!" said Shreya.

"But how the hell, they knew...!"

"That doesn't matter, anymore..." said Maya, she seemed lost.

"And what happened to you, Ravi...?"

"I rebelled and fought back, that's how I got the beating!"

"We failed badly...! Everything is lost!" said Maya.

"Don't worry Maya... we could still get Mayank, back!"

"How...! Shreya, How? We lost everything, we lost him...!" she said, crying.

"Inspector Anand... what you say!"

"I don't know, also...!"

"Sir... I say we kill all of them!"

"No... Tavde! They are too many, even if we got successful in freeing ourselves, we still can't overpower them... and I can't even call for Back-Up"

"What do you think; they are going to do with us...?"

"Of course...! They will kill us!" "No way, they will let us leave from here alive!"

"Yeah...!" "Riya is right...! We are dead!" said Shreya.

"I think we should still fight... for ourselves, and those kids!"

"But how... Manisha, we can't even save ourselves, let alone the kids!"

"Try to free yourself...!"

"Does anyone have a knife!" Riya asked.

"I had but, I think they took it..." Tavde replied.

"They also took... our guns, phones, and every other thing!" Anand said.

"So, I think it's time again to break my thumb!!!" said Maya.

"You are not going to do that, again!"

"Yes... Ravi is right!" "Last time we were at a different time, that's why you had to do that! Not this time!"

"But why not...! I did it last time... I could do that again!"

"Last time... it was our luck, your hand got healed, No! I will do it this time!"

"Are you sure...Riya?"

"Yes... I am!"

"But why...! I did it once, I could do it again..."

"Shh... someone is coming..." whispered Shreya.

"Take her, and that one..." said one of those men in robes.

"Where are you taking her...?" screamed Maya.

THE RITUAL (PART-1)

"Where they could have taken her...?" asked Shreya, panicked.
"I don't know...!" said Ravi.
"But why? Maya and Riya, only..."
"No idea!"
"Anand...! Do something!"
"Wait... I am thinking!"
"I am doing it... I am dislocating my thumb!" said Ravi.
"No..! Don't...!" screamed Shreya, but it was already too late, it was done. He freed all of them, one by one and then they left the room to save Riya and Maya. They saw that they were taking them to the execution table, put Riya's head on it and the man raised his Machete.
"You sick Fuck!" said Ravi and, kicked the man with the machete.
"Are you okay!" asked Shreya, freeing Maya. I freed Riya.
"Yes... I am fine".
"Me too...!"
"How did you..." Riya was saying when she saw his hand.
"You shouldn't have!" she said.
"And what...! let you die...Never!"
"Thank you..." she said, with a smile.
"I have something to tell you..." Ravi said, looking into her eyes.
"What..." asked Riya.

"Guys...! A moment!" screamed Shreya.
"Huh, what...!" Ravi said, realizing that there was a fight going on.
"I am coming!" he said and kicked the man who was trying to strangle Shreya.

"Thank you!" she said, sarcastically.

Anand was getting punched in the stomach; Ravi got that man by the neck, while Anand punched him in the face. Riya was trying to choke someone, while Maya found her bat and she was maniacally swinging it at anyone that came near her. It was more of a scene from a comedy movie than an action one. Me... I was hiding under the canteen window; my eyes were on guns, locked inside. "Bad luck!" there was a lock on the gate; I needed something to break it. I saw the machete in one man's hands, trying to stab Maya in the neck. I slowly walked from behind and caught him by the neck, but he was stronger than I had expected, he pushed me and I fell back, hurting my elbow. It took me a couple of seconds to gather my strength together and then I attacked him again, but this time I strangled him by my stall until he became unconscious. As soon as that happened, I got the machete and started breaking the lock, after five or six tries it still didn't break, I needed something like a hammer, something heavy not sharp, I found out you can't cut a lock.

"A little help here...!" I screamed but no one was available.
"Move...!" some said from behind. It was Anand, he opened the lock by pins, yes you thought right; just like in a movie. He got the gun and air fired, telling everyone to stop

immediately. Everybody paused, whatever they were doing.
"Leave everyone alone... and surrender! I will only give you one chance, or you are dead!" shouted Anand.
"You stupid people... you think you could kill us; stop us! Fools!" said the man who was standing next to Ravi.
"Of course, I can...!" replied Anand.
"You are a fool, then...! We are immortal! You cannot stop us. You all came here to die!"
"But how are planning to do that, because it seems I have the advantage!" Anand said, showing him the gun.
"You Morons...! Idiots! You came here because he wanted you to come... and you did, just like a puppet!"
"He... who?" asked Shreya.
"He... the one and only true God, our God...!" "The Great... Almighty! Mammon...!" the man said, bowing down in his honor. They all followed him.
"What! Mammoth! Who is it?" asked Ravi.
"You stupid boy... How dare you! Made fun of our lord! Kill them!" he ordered and chaos started. They ran in front of the gun like it was a toy, Anand shot a couple of times but nobody got hurt, finally they took the gun from his hand and knocked him out with it.

"Where I am...?"
"You are fine! At least for now...Anand," I told him.
"You were hit on the head...! Do you remember it?" asked Riya.
"Yeah... I do! My head hurts!!"
"Of course... you are bleeding!" said Maya.
"I am fine...!" he said, getting himself together.
"We are in canteen...!" said Shreya.

"What are they trying to do, now...?"

"We don't know!" "They just tied us here, and left..."

"Did I kill someone... I remember firing!"

"No... I mean yes! You fired but nobody got hurt... It was like they were bulletproof!"

"Or IMMORTAL!!" said Riya.

"Don't be stupid... there is no such thing as immortality!" argued Shreya.

"Things we have seen by now... I don't know, what to believe or what not to!"

"Yes... she is right!" said Maya.

"Come on! Guys! Don't lose your mind now!! We need it, more than ever..."

"I mean it could be true...!"

"Not you! Anand, you too believe in this!"

"I am not saying, I believe but I can't deny it also..."

"So... how do we kill them now?" asked Tavde.

"I don't think we can..." said Ravi.

"This is bullshit! Guys!" shouted Shreya.

"Don't look at her, she has her problems in believing reality...!" said Riya.

"What do we do now...?"

"We are so dead...!"

"Yes... Ravi is right! If we can't kill them, can't arrest them, then we are dead...!"

"We have to get out of here! Leave it! We need to save ourselves..." said Riya.

"She is right...!" Spoke Shreya from behind.

"Are you mad...? What about Mayank and those children!"

"We can't leave them here to die...!" said Maya.

"Think clearly... and don't be stupid, Maya...!" "How do we

know for sure, if Mayank is not already dead...?" "We can't risk our lives on uncertainty... and even if he is alive...how are you planning to get him back! Don't be stupid in love, or we all will die!"

"Are you crazy? Riya, like we talked we will find a way to get him back, by reading that book!"

"And where is that book...? Tell me!" Shreya interrupted.

"She has become a fool, or maybe she was from always... Guys! We have to save ourselves; I don't want to die, not like this, murdered by some stupid, delusional people!"

You don't care for anybody but yourself...! You have been like this always..." "And you too Shreya, that's why you two get along, so good...!" "What love...huh? What love! You are trying to say, I want to save him because I love him..." Maya screamed like she finally lost it.

"Shut up! Guys...!" said Ravi. Neither Shreya nor Riya said a thing.

"We need to work together...! If we want to get out alive!" said Anand.

"Yeah... he is right!" "So... for some time, just doesn't fight to each other... if you want to fight, fight them! Understand!!" said Ravi.

"Fine..." said Shreya.

"Hmm..." Riya said. Maya didn't say anything, but she was sure she didn't want to fight.

"Now we have to think, how to get out of here... I mean from canteen!"

"I already have broken my hand, and it hurts like Hell!" Ravi said.

"We won't need that... when they all were busy fighting, I hid this!!" said Tavde, showing us a pocket knife.

THE RITUAL (PART-2)

"Ohh...you came out on your own, Perfect!" said a man looking at us, as we came out.
"Yeah...you saved us, some trouble!" spoke another.
"Come... everything is ready for our Chief guests!"
"Huh...what Chief Guest...?" Maya asked.
"You all are...!"
"What do you mean?" asked Shreya.
"Sit and we will talk... Please sit..." said a man, indicating us to sit on specific chairs, there were five of them. We all sat, but there were seven of us and only five seats.
"Scoot over... for me!" said Ravi, sitting on Riya's seat.
"There is no space...!"
"So... where do I sit?" Ravi asked the man.
"The seats are for them... not you!" said the man, pointing towards Anand and Tavde.
"Move...!" another one shouted. They immediately got up.
"But why us...only?" asked Shreya.
"You are our guests, five of you! Not them!"
"Why... what is special in us?"
"Wait... we better show, you!" said the man, indicating another one to do something.
"What are you going to show...?" I asked, getting scared, we

all were a little scared.

"Wait...!"

"What the hell! Is that...?" said Shreya, as we saw two men, bringing a coffin on their shoulders.

"Please... sit down!" said the man to her.

"What is that...?" I asked, also getting up from my seat.

"Please, sit... I said sit!!!" the man shouted at me.

"Don't you try anything...!" said another man from behind.

"Mind your language...! They are our guests!" he ordered, it was like he was the leader.

"Show them...!" he said, indicating for them to open it.

"What the hell!!"

"Holy shit!"

"Is it real...?"

"He looks real...!" said Ravi looking at the coffin, inside it was a body of (what looked like a man) completely naked and with sewing marks on his whole body.

"Of course, it's real!" said the man.

"What...!" screamed Maya.

"Who is he...?" asked Anand. Tavde was too shocked to speak.

"He...well! He is a very old man if you really, want to know..."

"But he looks young...?"

"He was young, once... but anymore!"

"What... what do you mean?" I asked.

"Ohh... My God!!!"

"What is it...Maya?" "Are you all right?" asked Shreya, holding her up, she was about to fall, and she burst into tears.

" What is it Maya...?" asked Riya.

"Speak... for God's sake. Say something!" Ravi said, looking at her helplessly but she just froze.

"What is it...?" Anand asked, looking strangely at her.

"Say something...!"

"He...He..." she finally spoke.

"What... he?"

"He is Mayank...!" she said in one go leaving all of us too stunned to speak.

"What the hell are you saying!"

"No...He is not!" said Ravi.

"No, Ravi... she is right!" said Riya, getting down on her knees in shock.

"What...! Are you mad?" "I know my friend...He is not him!" Ravi said.

"Look carefully... it is him!" said Riya pointing towards the body.

"No...No! That can't be possible...!" Ravi said bursting into tears. I was shocked too but I didn't know how to react.

"Are you all sure...?" I asked.

"Yes... it's him!" said Riya.

"But how...?" Maya got the courage to finally ask.

"We, of course...! Didn't know his name, it doesn't matter..."

"And for how! We aren't the ones... who put him in; we are the ones who dug him out.

"What do you mean...?"

"We dug him out from where he was buried..." "In sixteenth-century... there were people known as 'Ilahmas', they are the real ones who caught him not us!"

"You mean those naked strange-looking people...?" asked Ravi.

"How do you know about them...?"

"Just tell me...!"

"Yes... them! The original worshippers of 'Asmodeus'" "We

are just finishing, what they started!" the man said with a smile.
"But why him...?" Maya asked crying.
"We don't know that...!"
"Is he dead...?" Shreya asked.
"Yes... for now! He is..."
"What do you mean... for now?"
"See...that's what I was telling you!" "Your friend here was... the first one in 'The Ritual', he will serve as The Host"
"Host for what...?"
"Our lord...!" "To bring him into this world, we need a human body as a host, and we need five other people to complete the Ritual..."
"Five...!" Riya said in shock.
"You mean us...!"
"Yes, my dear... you are the lucky ones, who will help Lord 'Asmodeus' to come into our world".
"Who the hell is he...?" shouted Ravi.
"You Bastard...!" said one man, bringing out his machete, then got stopped by the leader.
"Well... I can't explain his greatness; people have known him since the beginning of time. He is known by all by different names; some call him Asmodeus (like us), some call him Lucifer, the prince of darkness, father of lies, Beelzebub, Moloch, or simply 'Satan'..."
"You guys mean, the Devil...?"
"Yes...him!"
"Are you crazy...?" screamed Ravi.
"Are you out of your mind... you can't bring him on earth!" said Riya.
"Of course, we can, and we will... you will see for yourselves!"

"You all are sick...mentally Sick!" said Shreya.

"People have called us by multiple names throughout time... but it never stopped us! And never will, we will bring him, will finish what 'Ilahmas' started centuries ago.

"What... what about the children...?" asked scared Maya.

"They...! We needed gifts for our lord... they were just gifts 'Welcoming Gifts!" "Years ago we did its first part but we had to stop because of this special night 'The Blood Moon'... finally after centuries of wait... it is now upon us!" "Hail Lord Asmodeus!!" he screamed, every one accompanied him.

"But why so manychildren...?" asked Anand.

"We thought... the more the better!" "Our lord will be happy... seeing so much innocent blood spilled".

"You people have lost your minds...!" said Ravi.

"We will see that...!" said the man; he was as calm as a sea after the storm. No regret or fear on his face but a smile.

"So... it means we are the sacrifice...!"

"Yes, my dear... you are smart! You will become the brain of the Lord!"

"What do you mean bybrain...!" Shreya asked.

"The Ritual...! As I told you, we need a host and five other people; they will become part of The Lord's body".

"Start preparing them...for The Ritual!" he ordered and they dragged us inside the school.

THE BODY

"What are you doing...Stay away from me!" Riya said, kicking the man who was trying to put some powder over her face.
"What are you going to do...?" Shreya asked.
"You people are insane!" screamed Ravi.
"Stay away from me!" screamed Maya, pushing one man.
"Sick people... don't touch me!" said Shreya.
"Don't test our patience...!" said the man slapping her. "We are ordered to not harm you; otherwise I would have shown you my power...!"
"Please stop... you don't have to do this!" said Maya.
"What are you going to do with us?" Anand asked the leader, we were still on the ground; they only took five of them.
"Leave me alone...Bastard!" shouted Tavde, trying to loosen the man's grip that was holding him.
"We have something special for you... A Surprise!" said the leader.
"What is that...Tell me?" asked Anand.
"Wait...my friend!" said the leader, with a big smile.
"I am not... your friend!" said Anand in anger.
"They are ready...!" said one mancoming out of the room.
"Very good...The Eclipse is on us! Let's start the Ritual!"
It was around 1:30 in the morning, but for us, it was a bloody night. It was not your usual stay at home watching Netflix

weekend. It was a bloody horror movie, serial killer behind you, weekend. They brought us outside in the pinkish night; it was too late for us to run. Anand and Tavde were standing, as we passed by them we saw fear in their eyes and they might have seen it in our eyes. Maya was crying, and strangely Riya was crying too, I never took her for the crying type. I was scared too but after the incident with my sister, I just don't cry anymore. Shreya was cursing at them while Ravi; well, was not in his right mind, since he saw Mayank's body.

They placed us on different beds, laid down in front of Mayank's body. We were forced to drink something which made our minds foggy. Five men were standing beside each one of our beds with knives in their hands. They were going to open us while we were alive and took out our important organs. Heart of Maya (a kind heart), Brain of Shreya (a smart brain), Riya's Lungs (as she never smoked), Ravi's liver (perfectly healthy, because he never ate fried foods), and my eyes (as I had seen the death of myself). According to me, Ravi's body would have been more perfect than Mayank's, if you ask me. They chose Mayank because he was most abused in childhood, then all of us combined.

"Please don't do this...!" Shreya pleaded.
"Stop...are you nuts!" shouted Maya.
"Please...please...don't do this...to us!" Riya begged.

"You will not getaway, with this...!" I screamed on his face. They started the procedure to operate them while they were still alive but not in their senses because of the drink. Before they could do that, Anand somehow managed to get loose and get a hold of the gun, he fired in the air and everyone stopped. "I will shoot everyone dead if you didn't stop..." shouted Anand, pointing the gun towards the leader.

"Hahaha..." smiled the leader and everybody else.
"I am dead serious...I will shoot you!"
"Go on...shoot!"
"I will shoot you...!" Anand shouted again.
"Yeah...go on. Shoot!" said the leader with a smile.
"As you wish...!" Anand said and cocked the gun and 'BAM!!!' (Gun fired).
"Ahh...!" Anand screamed in pain, as he got shot. He turned back to see who shot him and couldn't believe his own eyes. He saw Tavde, standing with a gun in hand.
"But why...?" He asked, he got shot in the shoulder.
"You stupid person... you just don't give up!" said Tavde. "We tried everything, even tried to kill you but somehow you still managed to be alive, why didn't you just leave the case...as commissioner told you. Raka was sent to kill you, and I was sent to kill him, to not leave a trace behind. That idiot...missed a clear shot...!" he said in a frustrated voice. "I had to kill him... so he doesn't open his mouth," Tavde said in anger.
"We are everywhere... we are in the system... We are the system!!" "You can't touch us..." shouted Tavde, then laughed loudly.

He shot him again, and this time Anand fell to the ground. As his eyes closed down, he saw them start cutting us. But that didn't happen exactly like that, he started cutting but a gust of air pushed all of them back. Air was flowing furiously like a storm coming towards us, I wasn't fully lucid then but

I saw children, a lot of children. Coming towards us from all directions, they were hurt, some had bruises all over their bodies and some had markings on their faces, but they all had one thing in common, a cut mark on the throat like that's how they died.

They came near us and looked at us, all together, then walked past us towards those men, as they were behind my head and I couldn't turn, I couldn't see what happened, then I passed out.
"Where am I...?" I asked, gaining consciousness.

"We are saved... somehow!" replied Ravi, with a happy smile.
"But how...?" I asked.
"We don't know, but I think someone saved us...!" replied Shreya.
"Yes... I saw children walking towards us...!" said Riya.
"Yeah... I saw them too..." I said.
"Where are those people... and Anand? Where is he?" "What happened to him...is he fine?"
"No...unfortunately, we lost Anand..." Maya said, looking down.
"What...!" "And those people... where are they?" I said.

HIS ARRIVAL

Those people were still alive, even after the encounter with ghosts; maybe they were really 'Immortal'. Ghosts of the children saved us, but not for too long, we were not still fully lucid. They woke up and restarted the ritual once again, this time they finished it. Yeah... you got it right! I became blind and others were dead, while Tavde also got involved with them. That was all I saw before I heard screams of my friends, as they opened them alive and took out their organs, then it was my turn, I was scared to death but couldn't move, my body was paralyzed but I could still feel the air getting tensed around me, as he came above me with a knife in his hand, my eyes were hurting because of not winking. Tears started coming, could feel them flowing down my ears, could see a knife coming just above my eyes, I was shaking inside but my body was like a corpse, no response at all. I felt the sheer pain and coldness of the knife, as he inserted it in my eye, I could feel him scooping out my eyes, the pain and fear were indescribable. I felt when my eyes left eye sockets, and when he cut nerves connecting the eyes to the body, soon I was completely blind, and all I could hear was silence and my heavy breathing.

I was still feeling pain, but it wasn't hurting anymore, it kind of fell numb. Though I could feel something warm flowing down the same direction as tears, it was something dense and warmer; it was blood coming out of my eye sockets. I still couldn't move and my heartbeat got so fast, I passed out.

When I woke up, I was still blind but I heard people talking.

"The body is ready...!" said one person.
"It's time to finish The Ritual, and bring the Lord to earth..." said another one.
"What time is it...?"
"It's 3:00 am, the time of Evil...!"
"Let's start then...!"
"Everyone, circle the Body!" shouted the leader.
"What to do with them...?"
"Leave them for now... after Ritual, we will dispose of their bodies..."
"Okay...!"
"Everything ready...!"
"Yes...!" shouted everyone in unison.
"Bring the book...!"

Then they started chanting in some strange language and beating drums maybe. All I could hear was the beating of drums and their chanting.

"Ooo mighty one...! The Father of lies...! The prince of Hell...! Asmodeus...!" "We call you by your name... come to us, and show us the real power and wealth...! Come to this realm and made it yours...! Your servants call upon you... Ooo Lord Asmodeus! Come! Come! Come!" shouted someone, maybe the leader; it was hard to recognize his voice in all

those beating sounds.
"He is here...! Look!" shouted someone.
"The Lord is here...finally!"
"He is with us...!"
"Ooo my Lord... we bow down to you!" said someone.

I don't know who came and from where, but I felt the air getting heavy with a rotten smell in it and the fear, I had never felt fear like that before, not even when I saw them scooping my eyes. This fear was different, indescribable, slowly rotten smell increased, like dead bodies were around, which of course were. But this smell was not coming from a particular direction, it was all around, then everything went pin-drop silence, I could hear my breathing as well as theirs. I heard a footstep, and my heart fell into my stomach, I started sweating heavily. With every footstep getting closer, my heart was ready to come out of my chest. The fear was so intense, for a moment I forgot my pain, then it started again, worst than before, I wanted to scream, to cry but couldn't, I never felt as helpless in my life, as I felt that night.

I had lost faith after what happened to my sister, but that night, I remember praying. I remember asking God, for help. I remember begging him to lessen my fear, to give me courage, without uttering a word, I asked for a lot of things.

I heard someone coming near me, touching my face, all over the body. This touch was different from any touch, I had ever felt, it was cold and there were not five fingers in (whatever it was) hand. I tried to count but couldn't, it was like ropes swinging over my body.

"Lord Asmodeus… Please come into the body, we have prepared for you…" said Leader.
"You did well…!" spoke someone in a very deep and powerful voice that sends a shiver down your spine.
"Thank you… My Lord…! We did it for you…" "We have your gifts… ready with us, for you…! Take them!" only the leader was doing the talking.
"After soo… long! Finally, I have arrived on Earth!" "I have waited for this moment for millenniums…!"
"Bring the gifts…!" the voice spoke.

Then I heard multiple footsteps coming in my direction, it was the children, this time they were fully lucid. The voice gave the leader something, which he was very thankful for, to show that he likes the gifts. Then one by one, I don't know what it did to them, all I heard were screams of children, painful screams, begging to let them go. After the screams everything went silent, it was probably now in Mayank's body. I prayed to God for death, I couldn't take the fear and pain anymore; I didn't want to know what was going to take place, next. But unfortunately, I didn't die, now I was able to move my fingers and my toes, I was regaining control of my body, but I didn't move because I was practically blind. The devil was here on earth with us, everything was doomed now, with no hope left I stayed lying there in my position.

Then I heard a sound of firing, I was wondering who would have come here at this time of the night and that too with Devil being here himself. Whoever it was, was coming straight to their death, I was praying that he or she leaves the premises on time.

"Are you alive…?" asked someone, a new voice.
"Yeah… barely!" I replied.
"Can you get up…?"
"Maybe…" I said, trying to move my body, for first it was heavy but slowly I got the hang of it.
"WH…who are you?" I asked, getting up with help.
"I am…Sandeep!" replied the voice.
"Who are you…?"
"Doesn't matter now… we have to leave…! Come on!"
"Where is everybody…?"
"I fired in the air to make them run, but there was nobody when I got here…!"
"What…! How…?"
"I don't know… maybe they left?"
"Did you see him…?"
"Who…?"
"The Devil…?"
"What…?"
"Yes… they were successful in bringing him here…! He was here…!"
"Oh my God…!"
"Let's get out of here before they come back…!"
"But… now that we know, he is here! We can't leave him… we have to do something!" Sandeep said.
"DO What!!" "Can't you see I have no eyes, and I don't think so you brought an army…did you?"
"No… I didn't, but still, we can't leave him here. He will destroy earth…and everything we love!" "We have to stop him…!" he said again.
"But where is everybody…?" I asked.

"I don't know…! We should hide…"

"I think you are right…!" "I am already almost dead… I lost my friends; so much innocent blood has been spoiled… I can't leave now!" "They should not die in vain…!" I said, gathering up my courage, which wasn't much left after meeting 'The Devil'.

"Leave me...! Leave me alone...!"

"What is it Sandeep...!" "Tell me...!" I asked as I heard voices and Sandeep's panicked voice.

"Leave me...! Where are you taking me?" Sandeep said, screaming.

"What is it...?" "Please tell me something...!" I said, moving my hands in the air to feel something.

MEETING THE 'DEVIL'

"Where are you taking me...?" "Run Manisha...run!"
"Where...!" "Where are you...? Sandeep...!"
"Who is it...? Leave me alone" I said, as someone grabbed me from behind.
"Ahhh..." I screamed as someone threw me to the ground.
"It's so Good... to meet you...!" said the gravel voice.
"Who is it...?"
"Your eyes... they are very good!" "I can see very clearly...! I can see your pain...suffering, you have suffered a long time... now it's time to put you out of your misery!"
"You... 'The Devil'!" I asked, sweating in fear.
"Yes... I am, He...!"
"What are you going to do with us...?"
"You have served your purpose...!" "Now... it's your time to go!"
"What...!" "What do you mean...?"
"This...!" said the voice, as he lifted me in the air by the neck.
"Leave me...!" "I said...leave me!" I said, trying to free myself. I started to see things, not as you see with eyes but I was merely seeing outlines, like drawings with pencil, not even black and white but only sketching. I saw him, finally, I saw him 'The Devil', he was in Mayank's body. I kicked him and he dropped me, on my left side were some people, trying to hold down a man from escaping their grip. Maybe he was

Sandeep, I couldn't make him in outlines only, but I was sure it was him. I crawled backward to get away from him, as he came near me and then someone caught me by the shoulder.

"Who is it...?" I asked.

"It's me, your sister...!" she said.

"What...! How...!"

"Don't be afraid, it's me...!"

"No...That can't be possible! You can't be here!"

"It's me Manisha..., Priya...!"

"Priya...!"

"Yes...it's me!"

"But you are dead...!" I said, getting scared.

"No! I am alive... remember they released me!"

"No... They didn't!"

"But you told everyone... I came back, alive!"

"I lieddddd... you never came back!" "They didn't let you go... they murdered you...!" I screamed and burst into tears.

"And who killed me...!" said Priya's changing voice, it was soft and with love before, now it was harsh and cold.

"Those men killed you...!"

"No... You killed me...!" "My sister killed me...!"

"No...No...! It wasn't me. I tried everything to get you back safe...!"

"But you are one... who got me in trouble! Remember!" "You wanted to be so brave and good human... if it wasn't for you, I would still be alive" "You started all this mess... because of you they kidnapped me, tortured me, and finally killed me...!"

"I wanted to be with you...! Please don't say that!" "I loved you...! You are my sister!" I said crying heavily.

"Don't call me your sister...!" "I am not your sister... you are my murderer!"

"No...! Please don't say that...!" I begged. "I didn't testify... for you I came back!"

"You have to die, now...!" Priya said.

"No... Please don't kill me!"

"I am not going to kill you... you are going to kill yourself!"

"What...!!"

"And guess what...! I have friends with me!" Priya said, sarcastically.

"What!!!"

"Yes... you are a bloody murderer!" "You kill people... you kill these too! Just like you killed me...!" Priya said, and other figures emerged from behind her.

"You killed us...too!" said someone in the girl's voice.

"Who are you...?"

"I am Maya... did you forget me, so soon!"

"What...? But you are dead!"

"Yes... because of you!"

"Because of you!" said a male voice.

"Because of you!" said another male voice.

"If you had just told us...! We would be still alive!" said another female voice.

"You killed us...!" said all voices together.

"You killed us...!" they were coming towards me, now.

"You killed us...!" with Priya.

"I didn't kill you...!" "I didn't kill you...!" I screamed multiple times.

"I didn't kill you...!" I screamed again, and just like that, there was no one. Everyone was gone. I saw The Devil with Sandeep in his hands, maybe he was crushing him.

"Leave him alone...!" I screamed and ran towards him, other men caught me and I pushed them behind, I picked up the machete, and stabbed a man in the stomach. He screamed in pain, I couldn't stand blood but that day I saw a splash coming out of him and he fell. This was the first time I hurt someone in my life, let alone killed.

Then another person jumped at me and I cut off his head. I saw it flying in the air and falling to the ground. Blood was splattered all over me, on my face. It had been too much, I am going to put it to an end myself.

Another man tried to come near me; I swung machete in from him, grunting in anger. Finally, after holding on so long, I lost it. I killed every single one of them, it was just me and The Devil, now.

"It's now just you and me...!" I said looking at him.
"You are better... than I had thought!" "I am offering you my companionship... come with me and we will Rule the World, together...!"
"I have nothing to do with you...!" "Get the hell out of my world!... or you will have to bear my wrath...!" I shouted on his face, soaked up in the blood for a moment I forgot whom I was talking to.
"Oh... you are brave!" "You remember... whom you are talking to?" "I am 'The Devil'... 'The king of hell...!" "I have been tormenting mankind, since the day it all began..." "I was here before you and I will be here even after you...!"
"So what...!" "We have God! He created you, he can finish you...!"
"You have no idea darling, what you are talking about...!" "There is no God...! I am the only one...!"

"No... You are not!" I argued.

"Ohh yes, I am...!" "I was here even before you people created God...!" "It is nothing but your mere delusion... you wanted to create something powerful, something you could blame for all your misery, pain, losses and...So you don't have to take responsibility for your doings!" "So you people created, God...!" "But nobody created me... I was always here from the beginning and I will always be here...!" "Nobody is coming to save you...!"

"You are lying...!" "This can't be true...!" I shouted.

"I am not lying... darling!" he said.

"NO!"

"Tell me why do your sister got kidnapped... not anyone else?" "You were trying to do good...! You were helping everyone and still, your sister got killed...That's because there is no God!"

"No... I don't believe you!"

"But I can help you...!" "I can give you your sister back...!"

"What...!"

"Yes, Darling... I can give you your sister back!" "I can give you your four friends back, who died tonight...!" "I can revive every one of the children that have ever died in this process!" "I can give you, everything...! So tell me!" "Would you come with me...?"

"I...I..."

"Yes my dear, come with me...!"

"I...I don't know!" "I don't know!" "I don't know!" I said, confused and tensed.

"Come with me...!" he said going backward and a portal opened behind him, I could see many people standing inside, but couldn't make their faces, as for me they were mere outlines.

"I don't know...!" I screamed again.

"There is nothing left here for you...!" "Everyone you loved has already died... your friends... your sister...your Parents...!" he said, still moving backward.

"You will give me my sister back...?" I asked.

"Yes my dear...see I have her here with me!" he said and pointed towards a figure behind him, as it came forward, I recognized, it was Priya.

"Come with me...!" Priya said, calling me towards her.

"I am so sorry...!" "I got you killed... I am so sorry!"

"Don't worry about that...anymore!" "I am here...with you! Come!"

"Please forgive me...Priya!" I said, folding my hands together.

"You are forgiven...! I forgive you...Manisha!" "Come with me and we will forever be together...!"

"Can you give my eyes back?" "I want to see her... I want to see my sister!"

"Of course Darling...! Anything you want!"

"Ahhh..." my head started hurting and I covered my eyes with my hands in pain. When I opened my eyes again, I could see everything normally.

"My eyes..! I can see...!" I cried in joy. "Priya...my sister...!" I ran towards her and hugged her tightly; I had missed this hug for so long. I never thought I could be able to hug her again.

"See I am here...!" Priya said, she was looking just like she did, the day she got kidnapped. That cute ponytail, which I made that day, that neatly ironed school dress, those shining shoes. Her brown eyes were lit with hope and joy like always.

Her smile. God...! I missed that smile, so much.
"Mummy and Papa would have been so happy to see you once again...!" "They loved you very much... after you! They lost all hope in life". "They were living but were not alive...!"
"I know...everything!" "Coming with me... mummy, papa will join us afterward!"
"Are they there, with you...?"
"Yes... look!" she said pointing towards the fire color portal, and they emerged out of nowhere, waving and smiling at me.
"Maa...baba...!" I said crying in joy.
"Come with your sister...! We will be a family again...!" they said.

"Yes darling...go reunite with your loved ones!" said the Devil, now with horns over his head, the stitches on Mayank's body were healing and had almost disappeared.

"Okay...I will come with you!"I asked, finally making up my mind and walking towards the portal with her. Just as I was about to go into it, someone grabbed my hand from behind. I turned to look who it was.
"Anand...you...!" I said in shock.
"Yes...!" "Don't go... they are not your family...she is not your sister!" he said.

DECISION

"Don't listen to him…Manisha!" Priya said, pulling my hand.

"No…! Listen to me; don't go… they can't take you without your free will…doesn't let them!"

"But I want my family back…! I want my life back…!" I insisted.

"They are not your family…Manisha!" "Your family is gone…it's not them!" Anand said.

"I don't know… I don't understand!"

"Don't listen to him…Come with me!" said Priya insisting, I go with her.

"Yes…she is right!" said The Devil.

"No…It has to be your free will. Don't agree with them…" he said, he was still holding my left hand tightly. While my right hand was in Priya's hand. They both were pulling me in opposite directions.

"Priya is gone…!" "Don't believe in her…Manisha!"

"I am confused…I don't know, what I should do…!"

"Hello Brother…!" said a voice.

"Vishal…!" Anand said, surprised.

"Yes… it's me, brother…! How are you…?" "I missed you so much….!"

"I missed you too… I miss you every single day!" "Not a day has passed in which I didn't miss you, since you have gone…!" Anand said, crying.

"I missed you too...brother!" "Come with me... and we will be together again...!"
"I am so sorry... Vishal...!" "I was your big brother... I was supposed to take care of you, but I failed my duty...I am sorry!"
"It wasn't your mistake...Bhai!" "Bad things happen... It wasn't you!"
"No...it was me!" "I should have waited for you...! I am sorry!" Anand said, sobbing.
"Don't blame yourself...Bhai!" "Come with me... and we will be together again!"
"I don't know...!"
"Believe me, brother...come!" Vishal said. This time Anand left my hand. He stepped forward towards his brother, leaving me with Priya. He hugged him and messed with his hair, they laughed, Anand seemed very happy.

"I love you...I have always loved you...you were the best little brother!" Anand said, smiling and touching his face. "But you are not my brother...!" "My brother is dead...!" he said with a cold face and kicked Vishal inside the portal. As he fell back, he turned into an ugly Demon, with tusks coming out of his mouth and horns in place of eyes. It was horrific.
"Right now... Manisha! Do it!" Anand shouted, looking at me.

"You are not my sister...!" "My sister is gone...!" I said and pushed it back, it also turned into a Demon with two eyes, one above another, vertically.

"Run...!" Anand screamed, grabbed my hand and we ran out

of the school. I looked back while running, 'The Devil' who was in Mayank's body, his skin started burning from different positions and he screamed so loud, my ears bled. The weather turned black from pink, the wind was now flowing like a tornado, making it hard to see, but I saw him falling on his knees and opening Mayank's jaws from both hands, until his cheeks got to tear up, and then a black thing came out of him, like smoke and screamed into my face and I fell from fear. Anand got me up and running again. Everything got sucked into the portal, even the whole school building; we got out on a verge of getting sucked.

I saw the school falling and everything getting into pieces. People and police came and an ambulance too, but there was nobody left to save by then, I saw everything going into a deep void, as the sun rose with its beautiful rays spreading all over us, I saw my hands inked with blood, in the morning sun. I looked at Anand, his face was black from the dust of falling debris with scratches on it and marks of tears, where the water made its way down to his chin.

It's been a month, but I still remember that bloody night, so many innocent people lost their lives that night. I lost my friends, new ones but they were my friends and good people, may God Rest Their Souls in Peace. People got suspended in the police department and criminals got caught, bodies of children got found buried in the school ground but nobody believed us, about what exactly happened that night. Only I know what happened, and these memories will stay forever with me. I never heard from Anand after that night, but I have heard that he left the police department, well; good for him.

The book Omayun police gave it back to me, as it was not a piece of evidence, because there was nothing written inside, only hundreds of blank pages. I still have it with me, hidden somewhere safe, where it will never hurt anyone again.

EPILOGUE

Today, here I am sitting in my new home, which I recently bought. I thought I needed a change; I am happy, as happy as one can be after, all that.

So, it was me Manisha Roy… thanks for listening to my story.
"Coming…!" I will be back my landline is ringing.
"Hello… who is this?"
"Hello…!"
"Hello… is anybody there. Please answer…!" maybe it was done by mistake.
"Hello…!" said someone on the phone.
"Who is this…?"
"You think you won…!" "No, my dear… you didn't!"
"Who are you…?"
"That doesn't matter…what matters is that Sandeep is still alive!"
"Sandeep…!" I heard that name after a long time, I forgot about him. He was with us inside the school, but he didn't get out or did he? I don't know.
"Who are you… tell me your name!"
"Mansukh never had a child of his own… he couldn't. So he asked for a favor from the Lord… that favor was 'Sandeep'!"
"The Lord's flesh and blood…!"
"Who are you…?"
"You know me my dear…!" said the voice, and hung up.